THE DEFIANT WIFE

THE THREE MRS BOOK 2

JESS MICHAELS

Every book becomes a reality thanks to a huge team of people. Thank you Mackenzie, who helps me find the right words in the right order. To my Mom and to Kelsey who catch whatever we miss. To Teresa, who gives me amazing covers. To Ana and Nina who help keep my online me together.

And to Michael, who is my best friend, my partner in crime, my business guru and the love of my life.

CHAPTER 1

Summer 1813

Phillipa Montgomery had expected a great many things in her life, but marrying a bigamist, nearly being murdered by him and then helping one of his other brides ready for her wedding... well, she never would have guessed that one.

Yet here she was, standing in the home of her late...husband? It was easier to just call him husband even though he never really had been.

She was helping adjust the beautiful white feather-and-pearl headpiece in Celeste Montgomery's hair while Abigail Montgomery fastened the pretty sapphire necklace Celeste's future husband had given her, the one that matched her eyes.

"You look so happy," Abigail said, the tightness to her smile mimicking the same emotions Phillipa felt as she looked at her friend.

Not because she begrudged Celeste her happiness. No one deserved it more! But just because happiness was a feeling that had fled from Pippa's life years before, thanks to Erasmus Montgomery and his bitter lies, and she was, she could admit, if only to herself...jealous.

"I *am* so happy," Celeste breathed. "I could not have imagined that when Owen knocked on my door not so very long ago and destroyed my world with news of Erasmus's duplicity that I could ever be so happy."

Pippa smiled, and this one felt less tight. Owen Gregory, the investigator hired by Erasmus's brother, Rhys Montgomery, the Earl of Leighton, was the best of men.

Pippa swallowed hard at the thought of the earl. Pushed at things she ought not think when it came to the man.

"I don't think anyone could have imagined *anything* that has happened to us all in recent months," Abigail sighed as she sank onto the settee in the dressing room. "Between finding out our supposed husband had multiple wives, to each being suspected of his murder, to then finding out he wasn't dead after all."

"And then he tried to kill us," Pippa added with a shake of her head. "And now he *is* dead and you are marrying again. It's a whirlwind." Exhaustion overwhelmed her at just the thought of it.

Celeste turned away from the mirror and faced the others. "Yes, all those things are truly terrible. I don't deny it. But I also don't want to forget that what we went through brought us together." She reached out and caught Pippa's hand, then motioned for Abigail to take her other. When she had joined their circle, Celeste smiled through tears. "I'm so lucky to know you both. To call you my friends, as close as sisters despite all the terrible things. So I can't regret any of the worst, as it has brought me so much happiness."

Abigail leaned forward to kiss her cheek. "And it will only bring you more, I think." She glanced at the clock on the mantel. "Gracious, we are almost out of time."

Celeste's cheeks flushed with pleasure. "I can hardly wait."

Pippa smiled at her eagerness and squeezed her hand. "I will go tell the vicar and Mr. Gregory that you are almost ready while Abigail puts on your finishing touches."

"Thank you," Celeste breathed with a smile that rivaled the sun.

Pippa slipped from the warmth of her friend's joy into the hallway and drew a long breath as she pulled the door shut behind herself. Her hands were shaking and she smoothed them along the silky skirt of her gown.

"Phillipa?"

She froze, still facing the shut door. That voice was one she had come to know very well. Too well, truth be told. She swallowed hard, tried to wipe all emotion from her expression and turned.

Rhys Montgomery, Earl of Leighton, stood in the dim light of the hall and her breath caught just as it always caught, from the first moment she met him. He was a beautiful man, there was no denying that. He was tall, very tall, at least a head taller than she was. He had dark hair that swept over his forehead in always perfect waves. And blue eyes. The deepest blue she'd ever seen.

He was never mussed, he was never out of place. No, he was too proper for that. Too serious, thanks to the hell his half-brother had unleashed upon them all. Although she thought Rhys...Lord Leighton...had probably always been a thoughtful sort of person.

His perfectly sculpted jawline tightened and those blue eyes flickered over her face. "Are you well, Phillipa?"

Because there were so many Mrs. Montgomerys going around lately, those in the inner circle had taken to calling the women by their first names, at least in private, to reduce confusion. But she would never get used to the way Leighton said *Phillipa*. It rolled over his tongue almost like a caress and made her stomach flip in ways that it most definitely should not.

"I'm fine," she gasped out with a forced smile. "I was just coming to assure the groom that the bride is almost ready for him."

He inclined his head. "And I was sent by said groom to check on the bride."

Her smile became more genuine. "Mr. Gregory is anxious, then."

"Very." A flutter of a smile crossed his lips and she swallowed at the sight of it. The man was truly handsome and she had no right to dwell on it so much. For too many reasons.

He cleared his throat. "Actually, I'm glad to have caught you alone. There is something we need to discuss."

Her heart rate ratcheted up a notch and she fought to keep that reaction from her face as she motioned him back up the hall toward the stairs. At least if they were walking side by side, he couldn't look at her so intently. "What is it?"

He paused, like this conversation was uncomfortable. "My brother's son."

Now she stumbled and he reached out to catch her elbow. The briefest of touches, gone the moment she was steady, but she felt it ricochet through her body just like his words did.

The son was not her child, though she had raised him since his mother disappeared. Pippa's former servant, a woman who had turned out to be a long-time lover of Erasmus Montgomery. His true love. They'd had a child, one Erasmus saw as a bargaining chip and who Rosie, the mother, truly loved even if she had made a series of terrible decisions that separated them.

But now Erasmus was dead. Struck down by Rosie, herself, who had promptly run away.

"Kenley," she breathed, trying not to think too hard about those chubby cheeks she adored. She had not seen the boy in weeks, though she regularly heard from the servants who had taken over his care.

Rhys flinched. "He named him...Kenley?" he asked, his voice cracking in a way that revealed emotion he didn't show on his angled face.

"Yes."

He shook his head. "That was our father's given name. Taken from our grandmother's maiden name."

"I...I didn't know. Turns out I didn't know much. But I am sorry for the grief all this has caused."

"I know you are, even if you needn't be."

She lifted her gaze and he held it for a moment. Everything else in the hallway melted away then. All that was left was him as he held her attention, as he made her forget that anything else in the world existed.

She blinked and fought to maintain whatever little dignity she had left. "I appreciate your kindness more than you could know, my lord. When it comes to the child, though, I could make arrangements to return to Bath. Everything will be topsy-turvy because of the wedding, but I'm certain I could be ready the day after tomorrow and be home before the week is out. I could prepare a full report on the boy, and we could find some kind of schedule that would suit you as to his health and well-being."

She expected him to agree and for that to be the end of it. She didn't exactly look forward to a return, but she had always known it was going to happen. She had responsibilities there, of course. She couldn't live in the fantasy land of London forever.

But to her surprise, he shook his head. "No."

Her brow wrinkled. "N-No?" she repeated.

"I need to assess the situation for myself."

She stared at him. "But you...you have so much to attend to here. I know your world has been turned upside down, Rhys..." She shook her head. "Lord Leighton. You cannot possibly spare the time for this."

"He is a child," he said, his gaze holding hers again. "His life and future are the most important matters I have to attend to. I could not focus on the more frivolous resolutions knowing that I had not dealt with this first."

Her lips parted at the passion with which he spoke about a baby he had never even met. Never known the existence of until just two weeks before. "You are truly a decent man."

His jaw tightened and those bright blue eyes flickered over her again. "Not very decent, I assure you." He straightened his perfectly placed jacket with what looked like discomfort and then began to move down the hallway again, forcing her to follow. "Will you accompany me to Bath?" he asked.

Her heart lodged in her throat and she had to swallow hard to have any hope of speaking. "Yes," she squeaked out. "Of course."

"I know you didn't come here with a companion," he said, and his gaze moved straight ahead as they went down the stairs together toward the parlor where friends were gathered for the wedding.

"No, I...it is complicated," she said. "I came here alone."

"Then I will hire someone to attend you on the journey," he said. "For propriety."

She almost laughed at the very idea but held back the unladylike reaction. At the door to the parlor, she stopped and said, "I'm not certain that propriety applies when it comes to me anymore, but anything for your comfort, my lord. I will be ready to return to Bath whenever you need me to be."

"Thank you," he said softly.

She inclined her head and touched the door handle. "We will discuss particulars later, I'm sure."

He nodded and she entered the parlor. He didn't follow, but she felt his stare on her as she walked across the room. Felt it burn into her back like a flame. And knew how careful she had to be, because the warmth of his fire was most definitely off limits to her. For now. For always.

Rhys took a long sip of the glass of champagne that had been forced into his hand for the toasts and twitched his nose at the tickle of bubbles it left behind. It was a festive drink and a festive occasion, and he was happy for the couple. He'd begun to consider Owen Gregory a friend, and Celeste—well, now she was Celeste Gregory, not Montgomery—deserved the love she had apparently found.

All the women his brother had destroyed were owed happiness and likely a great deal more.

His gaze flitted across the room toward Phillipa Montgomery. She stood with Abigail Montgomery and the bride, their heads together in serious conversation. God's teeth, but she was beautiful. He never wanted to see it so clearly, but how could one not?

There was just something about the woman. And it wasn't her mop of curly blonde hair that never seemed entirely tamed by whatever pretty style she wore, or the long expanse of neck that made a man want to trace it with his fingertips. It wasn't her green gaze that was filled with intelligence. It wasn't just her lovely figure or her bright smile.

All those things were wonderful, of course. Undeniable in their attraction. But there was something deeper that always made Rhys turn his head when she entered a room. Always made him track her like a hawk.

It was her spark. Despite the terrible situation the woman was in, there was always this light in her. Like a never-ending candle burning in her soul. Her mouth almost always held a little smile, like she knew a secret, even when she was at rest. How he wished he could ferret that secret out. Give her a few more secrets to make her smile like that.

Only...he couldn't. *Ever.* Because she was the widow of his brother. Well, she sort of was, if one ignored the bigamy. He couldn't ignore that, though. It had already destroyed his world. His future. His name.

And so for at least two dozen awful reasons he had to ignore the longing that tightened his chest any time Phillipa entered a room. He had to chastise himself whenever he woke hot and hard because of dreams of her. He had to stop memorizing her scent and the way she tilted her head back when she laughed.

"Leighton." Rhys's best friend, the Duke of Gilmore, stepped up beside him and joined him in looking over the threesome of ladies across the room. Gilmore's sister had been the latest target of Rhys's brother before Erasmus's death. Both the one he faked and the real one. Gilmore had hired Owen Gregory to look into the blackguard pursuing his sister's fortune. And when Erasmus had been presumed murdered, Rhys had hired him in turn to find the culprit.

Complicated, to say the least, but he was pleased that his friendship with Gilmore had not been damaged. He had few enough people he was close to, he didn't want to lose the duke.

"Gilmore," he said, and they clinked their glasses without drinking. Before they could speak, Owen Gregory stepped up to join them. Rhys smiled at him. "It was quite the ceremony. My most sincere wishes for your happiness. Mrs. Gregory is a wonderful woman."

"She is," Gregory said with a happy smile that felt like a punch in Rhys's gut. "I am the luckiest of men."

Rhys let out the air in his lungs. "Will you stay in London?"

"Yes. I intend on taking her away this winter and having her all to myself, but for now I have work to do. So we'll settle into my little home here and practice being newlyweds."

Once more, Rhys's gaze flitted to where it didn't belong: Phillipa.

"And what of you gentlemen? Now that the situation with Montgomery has been resolved, what are your plans?" Gregory asked.

Rhys shook his head. "There is little resolved for me, I fear. Only new problems begun. We can cover up the murder, and I will. My brother was, as far as the law is concerned, a suicide."

Gilmore grunted a sound of displeasure. "And it only took a few bribes and payoffs. Not that I blame you, of course. It was the most palatable story."

Rhys flinched. "None of this is palatable. But the specter of murder or suicide or anything else surrounding his death doesn't change that the world knows what he did before that end. They know about the multiple wives and the debts and the bad acts. There is much to resolve, both the public...and the personal."

Gilmore and Gregory exchanged a glance filled with concern on Rhys's behalf. "Can I help?" Gregory asked.

Rhys felt heat suffuse his neck, creep toward his face at the humiliation. "You've done so much to help already," he said. "And I appreciate your kindness, your counsel and your friendship, both of you. But what is left to manage is something I fear I must do alone."

Gregory looked as though he wanted to argue that point, but before he could his gaze moved toward the three Mrs. Mongomerys. Well, two Mrs. Montgomerys now, and one Mrs. Gregory. There must have been some communication between husband and wife that Rhys couldn't understand because everything in Gregory's demeanor changed. He relaxed, loosened. Rhys envied him for that.

"There will be time enough for maudlin reflection on my destroyed life," Rhys said, giving Gregory a playful shove toward his new wife. "Today is for celebrating. Go to her, as it is obvious you wish to, and don't give another thought to me."

Gregory tossed a grin over his shoulder and then did as he'd been told, moving toward Celeste like a thirsty man toward water. When he was gone, Gilmore sidled close and nudged Rhys with his shoulder.

"What exactly are you left to manage?" Gilmore asked. "I am not fawning over a new bride, so perhaps *I* can be of help."

Rhys sighed. "My first focus must be my nephew." He gulped at the idea. "That child should not suffer for what his parents did, not to themselves, not to each other. So we will go to Bath likely the day after tomorrow and I will see what is best in that situation."

Gilmore arched a brow. "*We*? Who is *we*?" Rhys was quiet for apparently too long because the duke answered his own question. "*We* being you and Pippa?"

There was something in his tone that made Rhys duck his head. "Don't," he growled.

Gilmore moved to stand in front of him so he could look him in the face and effectively block any attempt at escape. Because his friend knew him so well, damn him.

"I have been your friend for how long?" he asked softly. Gently, even.

Rhys shook his head and refused to meet Gilmore's stare. "I don't know. Too long. All my life. Long enough for me to tell you that I don't need your opinions."

Gilmore rolled his eyes. "Well, that's never stopped me."

Despite everything, Rhys couldn't help but smile at the quip. He relaxed a fraction. "No, I suppose it hasn't. And since you will do as you like without a thought for me, then go ahead and give them, but know I'll ignore them."

Gilmore snorted but his demeanor quickly became more serious. "Rhys," he began, and Rhys stiffened at the use of his given name. They never called each other by anything but their titles, not since they were in short pants. It gave a gravity to the situation that only piled up on everything else. "She is fascinating."

Rhys wrinkled his brow. He hadn't expected that to be what his friend said. *Fascinating.* Yes, that was the way to describe Phillipa, and a slash of jealousy was his immediate response. One he shoved down as hard and as fast as he could.

"Indeed," he said because Gilmore seemed to be awaiting some kind of answer to his statement.

The duke edged a little closer. "But if you are interested in her, and I say *if* even though I know there isn't an if about it…it could be bad."

The first reaction that hit Rhys in the chest was a strong desire to shove Gilmore away from him. Like distance would make what he said less true. That somehow he could erase this moment and pretend it hadn't happened.

But once that sudden and violent sensation passed, a more metered response settled into his chest. Gilmore wasn't wrong. An interest in Phillipa would be…bad. It *was* bad. There was nothing to do but fight it. Deny it to others and to himself until it went away. It had to go away.

He cleared his throat. "I am only interested in making things right for her and for the boy."

Gilmore lifted his brows. "So you say."

Rhys glared at him. "I am!" he snapped, with far more heat than the benign response warranted.

Gilmore raised his hands in surrender. "So you say," he repeated.

Rhys let his hand tighten on the half-full flute of champagne still gripped in his hand and drew a long breath. "And what about you?" he asked.

He noted that Gilmore's gaze slid back across the room to where Abigail Montgomery now stood alone. It flicked over her and his mouth tightened, for everyone knew the two despised each other.

"I am only an interested observer," he grunted. "There is nothing else for me here."

Rhys arched a brow, because he wasn't entirely sure that was true. Then he lifted his glass. "Then we are the same. Nothing of interest for us in the house of cards my brother built. So let us toast to the happy couple."

Gilmore clinked his glass without looking at him. "To the happy couple," he grumbled.

And they both drank without smiling, lost in thoughts of ladies who were out of reach by circumstance, by design, by whatever power made things impossible.

CHAPTER 2

Pippa entered the parlor, looking for her book so that she could add it to the ever-growing pile of things to pack for her return to Bath. She came to a halt as she realized Abigail was standing at the window, staring out at the fading afternoon sun.

They had been friends from the moment they were introduced, and Pippa had loved that fact. She knew some women would have hated each other in the circumstances they'd encountered. They would have fought over the blackguard who had betrayed them all, rather than stand together.

But Abigail hadn't done that. Neither had Celeste. Their bonds of friendship were strong and true. But tested recently. Pippa had found out that Abigail knew about the marriages before anyone else, and it had soured their bond a little.

Now Abigail looked at her and there were tears in her dark eyes. "I hate that you have to leave. Especially since I know you are angry with me."

Pippa crossed the room in a few long steps and wrapped her arms around her friend. "I was taken aback when I knew you had knowledge about Erasmus's behavior. I suppose I wished you had saved me the same way you tried to save Gilmore's sister from our husband's wicked clutches." She sighed as she guided her to the settee, and they sat together. "But you had no way to stop this any more than I did. It wasn't fair of me to react so strongly."

Abigail let out a small laugh. "As if any of this is fair."

"No, it isn't."

They sat in silence for a while until Abigail rested her head on Pippa's shoulder. "But doesn't it give you hope to see Celeste find true love? A future outside of this nightmare?"

Pippa shifted in discomfort. "It makes me happy for her, of course. But her circumstances are so unique. Owen knew all of us, knew what had happened, and never judged her. I doubt it will be easy to find another man with such an open heart. Especially since there are no longer dowries to make such a match palatable in other ways."

Abigail let out a sigh. "I know you're right."

Pippa sat up. "I'm sorry to be gloomy. I'm only trying to find a way to accept this for myself, but it is unfair to drag those burdens onto you."

"No, they are the same thoughts I have late at night, staring at my ceiling." Abigail shrugged. "It's as if...as if..."

"The future is just a blank page," Pippa whispered. "I've always been able to picture it, but now it's just...gone."

Abigail pulled a face. "God's teeth, that's a horrible idea. You can see some of a view of it, surely. You'll leave for Bath in just a few hours and you will have much to do there. You and Lord Leighton."

Pippa heard the shift in Abigail's tone when she said Rhys's name, and shut her eyes briefly. "You act as though we will be together during his time there. He has a great deal to manage—I'm an afterthought. He only considers me when it comes to what he believes he owes us all for his brother's actions, and for the good of his nephew."

"You think that is all?" Abigail asked, watching Pippa get to her feet and pace away.

"Of course it is," Pippa insisted, stopping before the fire and staring into the flames. "There could never be anything more to it, even if I wanted there to be. Lord Leighton needs to tidy up his reputation, connecting himself with me in any way would do nothing for that purpose. He needs to find a lady of impeccable actions and credentials. Someone who will make Society forget what Erasmus did, not remind them of it every time she enters a room."

"Pippa—" Abigail began.

Pippa shook her head and faced her with a smile that felt as forced as anything. "He will be here shortly, and I still have a great deal of preparing to do. Would you come help me?"

Abigail studied her a moment, then got to her feet. "Of course. I'd do anything you needed, love. Anything at all."

Pippa knew that was true as they linked arms and headed up to her chamber for the last gathering of items and checking of drawers and cupboards. That was the only way Abigail could help her now. The rest of what she needed to do and how she needed to behave rested entirely upon her own shoulders.

And she was determined not to fail or fall victim to a temptation that could never be.

Rhys's carriage arrived exactly on time a few hours later, and Pippa found herself watching as he chatted with the servants that had loaded her bags. He was very kind, jovial even. A few times he cracked a smile during the endeavor, and she was mesmerized.

Rhys hadn't done much smiling in the short time she'd known the man. For obvious reasons.

But at last everything was prepared and the time had come. He joined her and Abigail on the step for the farewells.

"Do take good care of her, my lord," Abigail said with a pointed glance in his direction that made Pippa blush.

"I will, Abigail," he promised as he took both her hands briefly.

"And you and I will have a great deal to discuss when I return. I have not forgotten you in all this."

Pippa turned away slightly. Unlike the other wives, Rhys had always known Abigail, for she was the only legal one in the bunch. The two seemed to share a casual friendship, and that was to be expected.

Still, there was something about looking at it that made Pippa's own heart throb a little harder.

"I know you haven't. We'll talk upon your return." Abigail pivoted to Pippa, tears in her dark eyes. "Oh no. I hate this. You must promise me you'll come back to London."

There was a wildness in Abigail's tone. A desperation that Pippa rarely heard from her. She nodded even though she wasn't certain she would be able to come back here for a very long time. "I will."

They hugged, both trembling as they clung to each other. Finally, Abigail released her and turned away. "Forgive me, I do not think I could bear watching you go."

She fled into the house, and Pippa lifted a hand to her mouth to catch a sob. She stared at the door Abigail left open in her haste, breath coming hard and heavy as emotion overwhelmed her.

"Come now," Rhys said softly, and she jumped when he took her arm.

She glanced up at him and her breath disappeared for a far different reason. He was staring down at her, face lined with concern and gentle understanding, and for a brief moment she wanted to turn into his chest. She wanted his arms to come around her. She wanted to breathe in the scent of him through his coat and know what his warmth felt like.

He darted his gaze away as if he could read those inappropriate thoughts and guided her toward the carriage. "I hired a maid for you, as we discussed," he explained as they reached the carriage door. "So be prepared."

She drew a gulp of air and wiped the tears from her cheeks. "I'm ready," she lied.

He squeezed her arm and then opened the door, helping her up into the vehicle. A petite young woman sat on the bench, and for a moment Pippa stared. Sit next to this stranger or across? Across meant she would sit next to Rhys. She didn't think she was ready for that.

So she slid into place beside the young lady as Rhys followed her into the vehicle. "Mrs. Montgomery, this is Nan Feeley."

"Good afternoon," Pippa said, extending a hand in greeting. "I so appreciate you taking on this position on such short notice."

"Of course, ma'am," the young woman said softly as they shook. "I'm happy to be of service to you."

The way she looked toward Rhys made it clear she knew who her true employer was, but what did it matter? She had a kind way about her, and it was true that Pippa needed a maid. Her last one had...

Well, her last maid had mothered a child with Pippa's husband, so there was that. She tried to push the bitterness of that truth away as the carriage rocked into motion and they headed onto the street.

"I'll ride along with you ladies for a while," Rhys explained. "Though I might change to my horse after a spell."

"The weather is beautiful for it," Pippa said, pulling the curtain back as the afternoon sun twinkled through the sparkling glass. "I don't think I can hardly recall a finer late summer in years."

For a while they discussed the weather, and she was pleased that Rhys had steered them that way. Surely Nan had heard of Pippa. He might have even had to pay her a little more to associate herself with such a fallen woman. But the topic of weather was benign and allowed Pippa to relax.

Except for when she looked at Rhys. Her foolish heart increased every time she was so wrong as to do that.

Eventually they rode from the confines of London, though, and the pace of their carriage increased. Nan reached for embroidery to pass the time, and that left Pippa to do nothing but stare once more at the man she'd been trying not to look directly at for an hour.

He smiled and his gaze slipped to Nan before it returned to her. His meaning was clear. Although he had hired the young woman and probably vetted her meticulously, she was still a stranger. They would have to be careful about what they spoke about in front of her.

"Are you pleased to return to Bath?" he asked.

Pippa pursed her lips. He probably thought that was a harmless question, as meaningless as the weather. She knew better. But she didn't have to reveal herself. Not to either of her companions. She was capable of small talk, after all.

"I grew up there," she said. "I know it very well."

His brow wrinkled a little at the nonresponse. Of course he would catch it. He was too clever and observant not to. "I've visited a few times," he said. "It is expected that one must go there to take the waters and see the sights."

She nodded slowly. "Yes, it is a busy town. There were many diversions to be had there thanks to the bustling tourist trade. My father benefitted, of course."

"He owns an…"

She filled in the gap. "Assembly room. A very popular one, at that. Visited by all of quality who come to the city. If you visited, you probably went there yourself."

That was a thought. The idea that Rhys had glided his way through the assembly rooms, that perhaps they had just missed each other, made her shiver.

She tried to keep her face neutral, but it was almost impossible. Worse when he said, "I think you must look forward to seeing your parents again."

She swallowed, tried to control her breath and her tone as she shrugged one shoulder. Yes, that was a nonchalant action. "I suppose one might think that."

He wrinkled his brow again and opened his mouth as if to press. But then he glanced at Nan. She was still sewing, but occasionally her gaze flitted toward Pippa. He shut his mouth and shook his head.

"It was an interesting experience growing up around such a place," she offered as a way to break the discomfort her answers had created. "Our little house was just behind the great hall, and during the high season, the music would float back so I could hear it." She smiled, for these memories were not unpleasant.

"And would young Miss Phillipa Windridge sneak a peek at those gatherings?"

She blinked. "You know my maiden name?"

He shrugged. "Of course."

"Of course," she repeated with a shake of her head. "And yes, I was always creeping up to windows and sneaking through the hall, hiding behind furniture so I could see what the fine dresses looked like, watch the dancing. By the time I had a dance instructor, I was already well-versed in reels and quadrilles."

"And the waltz?" he asked softly.

She blushed. "No, my father didn't allow anyone to waltz at Windridge's Assembly. He said it was too shocking, made a big bluster that those at Almack's gave permission for such a display."

"He was a stern master of ceremonies, then?" Rhys asked. Teased, she thought, gently and in a way that made her smile.

"Sometimes," she said. "He was very particular about attire and behavior in his walls. Any walls he ruled over."

Rhys nodded slowly, as if he understood that she was trying to tell him a little bit about life behind the assembly. In the little house where her spark had been seen as a disadvantage, a difficulty needing to be snuffed out by any means necessary. Where she'd been a commodity and a disappointment.

Nan had rested her head against the carriage wall now and was dozing. It seemed to give Rhys a little more bravery in speaking. "I'm surprised he allowed my brother into his hallowed halls if they were so well-protected."

Pippa swallowed, her mind taking her back to that night years ago when Erasmus Montgomery strode into the assembly hall. She was attending every entertainment by then, strutted out on display in the hopes she would land a man to elevate their station and bring even more prestige to her father's doors.

She'd been so stifled her entire life, and she recalled looking at Erasmus and thinking he was free. And she was jealous and intrigued. Enough that she ignored warning signs and the desperation laced in his pursuit.

"Erasmus was very good at presenting as a sheep when he was truly a wolf," she said. "And my father wanted to be taken in, so he was. I suppose..." She let out a soft sigh. "I suppose I cannot judge, though, for I was taken in, too."

Rhys's cheek twitched and his hand flexed against his thigh, as if he were considering reaching across to her. He didn't, of course. Unlike his brother, who had been impetuous and sometimes inappropriate, Rhys was always proper. Collected. And she respected that a great deal, even if the idea of him taking her hand sent a full-body shudder through her that was anything but unpleasant.

She was lonely, that was all. That was why her attraction to this handsome man was so powerful. Once she was home with her servants and Kenley, it would fade. She'd settle into her old routines and this drive would just go away.

She ignored the fact that her old routines had been unsatisfactory.

"I'm...sorry," he said softly.

She wrinkled her brow. "You are always so quick to apologize for something you had nothing to do with."

"Didn't I?" he asked, and his jaw twitched again. "I cut him off. Did that not set in motion everything that happened after? And since he is...he is dead, doesn't that make me the responsible party now?"

She flinched at the pain in his voice, the guilt and the grief that was just below this man's cool and collected surface. She'd always sensed it there when she spoke to him, always wished she could soothe it. But that was not her place.

"It doesn't make you responsible in my estimation," she said.

He held her stare a long moment, the bright blue of his eyes holding her captive. Then he cleared his throat and turned toward the window. "Seems we are out of London proper now. I always forget how long it takes. Perhaps it would be a good time to stop and stretch our legs, then I'll ride for a bit so you may have some time to get to know your new companion and enjoy the quiet."

She swallowed at how driven he was to escape her company, and yet she could do nothing but nod as he tapped the wall behind him to signal the driver to stop.

"There's a very nice inn along the road where we'll stop in a few hours," Rhys explained as the carriage slowed and pulled to the side. "And we will arrive in Bath before supper tomorrow."

She forced a smile. "That is fine. Thank you again for the transport and the company."

He bowed his head as the carriage stopped, and then ducked out, his deep voice fading as he spoke to the driver and made his arrangements. She reached into her reticule for a book, which she set on the seat across from her.

She needed to gather her senses and focus instead of mooning in an unseemly fashion over a man she could not have for a dozen good reasons. She had to. There was just nothing else to be done about it.

CHAPTER 3

R hys sat at a table in the dining hall of the inn where their group had stopped an hour before. He tapped his thumb restlessly on the wooden tabletop, rapping out a rhythmless beat as his mind spun in what felt like never ending circles. He didn't like feeling so untethered, so helpless. It wasn't in his nature—it never had been.

And yet he had no choice. The world was burning around him, set ablaze by a man he had spent a lifetime both loving and hating. Rhys was left to fight the fires alone, and the thoughts of that had plagued him the entire long day of riding ahead of the carriage.

Thoughts of something else, too. *Someone* else. The woman who had just entered the dining hall and was searching the crowd for him. He stood so she would see him better and sucked in a breath. Phillipa.

It was shocking how beautiful she was. Every man in the room made mark of it. He saw the eyes follow her, admiring the curves of her figure, the slope of her delicate neck, the bright, barely tamed glory of her golden hair and her lively green eyes.

But they didn't know her at all. They didn't know how far that beauty sank beneath the smooth surface of her skin. That she was just as alluring when she spoke or acted as she was to look at.

Wanting her was so very unfair. Knowing he could never have her was physically painful.

She smiled as she reached him, and he held out her chair for her. When she had settled into place, he said, "I hope you found your accommodations pleasant."

She nodded. "It's a beautiful room and a lovely inn. Much better than the accommodations I secured for myself on the way to London what feels like a lifetime ago."

He flinched because her words had made him picture her desperation, her fear, her suspicions when she chased his wayward brother to London. When the world was turned upside down by everything Erasmus had done and said and stolen.

"I wish I could have spared you that pain, Phillipa," he said softly.

She reached across the table and touched his hand. It was the briefest and lightest of touches, but he felt the warmth of her glide up his arm, through his blood, sliding into every part of him.

"Once again, it wasn't your fault." She shook her head as she rested her hand back in her lap and clenched it. "I don't know how to convince you otherwise when you are so eager to accept the blame."

He let out a long breath. "I suppose it is old habit. Trying to… prove my worth by never failing."

They were briefly interrupted by the serving woman, who explained the offerings from the kitchen. When they had made their selections and he had chosen a bottle of wine, the servant left. Phillipa met his gaze.

"Would you tell me a little about it?" she asked.

He grabbed for the bottle the girl had left on the table and opened it before he answered. "About my family? My life?"

She nodded. "You know a great deal about me. I'm sure you had many reports from Owen. Thorough ones."

"Not as thorough as you might think," he muttered, because he had pored over those very reports after he met her and always longed for more information about her, more personal connection he could cling to. "But I understand your meaning. The fact is that you are the victim of a very long story that culminated in my brother's death. And you deserve to know why, I think. Deserve to see a layer peeled back after so many of your own have been exposed."

She pursed her lips as if to disagree with that statement, but her curiosity must have gotten the better of her, because at last she nodded.

He drew a breath, poured the wine and took a long sip. "The last Earl of Leighton, my father, was a complicated man. He had married my mother by arrangement almost the moment she came out into Society and got her with child nearly as quickly."

Phillipa shifted at the delicate topic. "They must have had a great passion for each other."

"On the contrary," he said with a shake of his head. "I think the earl simply wanted to dispatch his duty as swiftly and efficiently as possible so that he could set her aside and get on with his life."

"That must have been difficult to watch."

He took another drink of wine. "I'm sure it would have been. Only my mother died when I was just two years old. I don't remember her. I only know what she looks like thanks to a portrait done of her as a wedding gift to the couple. My father hid it in an attic, but it now hangs in my hall at Gramtham Hills, my estate in Leighton."

"I'm so sorry. I knew your mother died—Erasmus always mentioned you had different mothers—but I didn't know it was when you were so young."

Rhys shrugged as though it didn't matter, even though that wasn't true. "Within six months of her death, my father remarried. Erasmus's future mother, a woman who despised me because I would take what she felt any children of hers were owed. She was never friendly, insisted I call her Lady Leighton or my lady."

"But you were just a child," Phillipa breathed. "How could she not look at you and feel warmth or connection?"

He was happy for the interruption of the server bringing their supper. It allowed him to gather his thoughts, control his emotions. It was something he'd always been good at, but the ability frayed when he was around this woman.

When they were alone again, he snagged her stare. "Like you do with my brother's son?" he asked. "Do his connections, the fact that he is proof of a betrayal...does it not bother you?"

She was the one to drink now. "I won't say I wasn't devastated when I realized he was your brother's illegitimate son. But that is not his fault. And now when I look at him, all I see are pudgy cheeks and a sweet smile. All I want is to protect him and to make certain he is happy."

He held her gaze for a long moment, and then he choked out a breath that he hoped sounded more like a laugh than a sob. "Well, you are twice the woman than Lady Leighton was. She only got worse when she bore my father his second son, his spare. She doted on Erasmus and froze me out of their family circle all the more."

"Your father had no drive to protect you?" she asked.

"If he had been indifferent to his first wife, he seemed quite the opposite with his second. He adored her and their child. They were the family of his heart and he allowed her free rein to treat me as she saw fit. All he cared about was that I was properly trained to become earl. When I dared complain about her coldness when I was ten or eleven, he stuck me so hard my ears rang and told me that I should thank her."

"Thank her," she repeated, her voice trembling. "For what?"

"That she wasn't making me soft," he said. "He told me competition was good for a man, including competition for affection. That I never won the day was a reflection on me, not on my stepmother or my half-brother or him. I had to try harder."

"I am so very sorry," she said, and touched his hand again. This time she let it linger, and he stared at her fingers draped across his flesh. She removed them again, this time with a blush.

"What is it you keep saying to me?" he asked. "That I should not apologize for actions that weren't my own?"

"I can still be sorry it happened to you," she said. "Because you didn't deserve such terrible neglect. You were a child—your family should have been driven to protect and embrace you."

"As yours did?" he asked.

She worried her lip, and he made a show of eating both to put her at ease but also to catch up since she had been eating as he spoke while he had hardly touched his own food.

"My father wished for a son to further his fortunes. I was a disappointment, but one he felt he could still benefit from, if only I were molded properly," she said. "So if yours harmed through neglect, mine did the same through an excess of intrusion. They poked and prodded and told me I had to change, do better, be better...until I managed to marry the second son of an earl."

He shook his head. "Great God. And what a mess that turned out to be."

"Oh, yes. My father wrote me in a rage while I was in London. He blamed me for what Erasmus did. He...he cut me off. That is why I was loath to speak about them in the carriage."

He flinched. Here he had hoped he was returning Phillipa to a loving family who could support her in this difficult time. But it seemed he was not the only one alone in the world.

And yet they were the two people who couldn't reach for each other for comfort.

"I ought not have pried," he said, pushing his half-eaten food aside.

"Why not? I certainly did," she said.

"But you are owed answers. My brother lied."

She wrinkled her brow. "Yes, he did. Often and with great talent. But you never do."

There was something in her tone that made him focus all the

harder on her. They locked stares, and for a moment it felt like everything in the world faded except for this woman. This *remarkable* woman.

"I'm sure I must," he said, hating how rough his tone sounded to his ears. Rough with desire, would she mark it? Would she hate him for it?

"No," she whispered. "Not that I have ever seen. You are...*good*, Rhys." His stomach flipped at the use of his first name. "And what you are forced to clean up is not fair," she finished.

He shook his head as he pondered that. The concept was one he'd done a great deal of thought about the last few weeks and months. "Life isn't fair."

"Don't we both know it," she said.

He wanted to touch her then. Not take her hand, which could be construed benignly enough, but stroke her cheek. Cup her chin. Draw her into his lap and put her arms around her. Just feel that she was real. Pretend that she was his. An illusion that would vanish when the sun hit it, but who cared? For the moments it felt true it would be amazing.

He blinked and broke the spell. "We have an early morning and it was a long day," he said, setting his napkin on the tabletop. "Perhaps I should escort you up?"

She dropped her gaze from his. "I think that would be best."

She stood and he followed her. He wanted to offer her an arm, but didn't. They walked together, never touching, across the dining hall and through to the stairs that led to the chambers above. She pointed in the direction of her own and stopped in front of a door that was just three down from his own.

So close. Yet so far away.

She managed to look at him again, though she did not meet his eyes. "Thank you for the company," she whispered, her voice barely carrying even in the narrow hall. "And for the kindness."

He inclined his head. "You will always have it. Good evening."

"Good night," she said, and then turned away, disappearing into the room.

He stood staring at the door for a long moment before he managed to get his feet moving toward his chamber. As he staggered inside, he let out the curse that had been clogging his throat for the entire night.

"Bloody fucking hell."

The scent of Phillipa was still in his nostrils, he could almost feel the pressure of her fingers on his hand. He wanted, more than anything, to go back to her door, haul her into his arms and learn her taste. He wanted to drown himself in her body until he didn't even remember all the good reasons that kept them apart.

But he couldn't, so what he was left with was a rising erection and a longing that would never be quenched except in fantasy.

Which he would indulge in now.

He crossed to the bed and flipped the placard of his trousers down with a flick of his wrist. His cock, half-hard from thoughts of her, bobbed free and he caught it, stroking the length as he leaned against the edge of the high mattress. How he'd love to have her here, watch her fingers clench the coverlet as he undressed her. Feel her backside push against him in invitation.

He spit on his hand and stroked himself harder, arching his hips like he would if it were Phillipa he was claiming. He'd be out of control if he touched her. He would grip her hips, grind her back against him as she panted and keened.

And he would make her come. With his tongue, with his fingers, with his cock. He would make her come over and over until she was slick with sweat. Until she was shaking with the exertion of it.

He was close to orgasm now, and hurried. With her, he wouldn't. He would take his time, but fantasy allowed for selfishness and he squeezed his eyes shut as he pretended it was her tight, wet body that gripped him. Pretended she was crying out his name.

Rhys. Rhys. Rhys.

He could almost hear her voice saying it, like she'd said it at supper. Almost feel her legs locked around his hips.

He came in great heavy spurts, collapsing against the edge of the bed with a gasp. It had been some time since he allowed himself this pleasure.

He rested his head on his forearm as his heart rate returned to normal. As fantasy faded and was replaced by cold, hard reality.

What he wanted he could not have.

This wasn't the first time that statement was true. It likely wouldn't be the last. The best thing he could do was stop torturing himself like this. It was no good to anyone.

Pippa leaned back on the door, her hands shaking and her mind racing as she heard Rhys's footsteps move away at last. And yet the troubles he created in her body and her heart and her soul remained as if he were still there looking into her eyes.

The Earl of Leighton was her late...

Well, she couldn't quite call Erasmus her husband, could she? Their union wasn't legal, it wasn't binding, it wasn't true. But the man had been her lover. At one point she'd even thought she loved him.

So wanting his brother now was...unseemly. Wrong.

"I can't do this," she whispered, as if saying it out loud would somehow make her understand it better.

"Ma'am?"

She jumped because in her distraction she hadn't even noticed that Nan was lying on the narrow bed near the fire. She'd been sleeping, it seemed, and now she got up, eyes bleary and concerned.

"Nothing," Pippa gasped. "Just woolgathering. I'm sorry, I didn't mean to wake you."

"Not at all," Nan said. "The travel just puts me out of sorts and I dozed off while I was reading my book. Did you have a nice supper?"

"Yes," Pippa said, and it wasn't a lie. "But I think the travel has affected me the same way it has you. Will you help me undress? Perhaps I'll try to sleep a little early, too."

Nan nodded and hustled to do her duty, chatting away as she did so. Pippa half-listened, nodding and making sounds of support. But in truth, her mind wandered to her time with Rhys. To the feelings he inspired just by being near her.

And to the fact that none of it mattered. She had to let this go. And she had to do it soon.

CHAPTER 4

P ippa drew a deep breath as the carriage slowed to a stop. She had a few moments before the door was opened, and she needed to gather herself so that she could pretend everything was fine and normal.

It had been a long morning of travel since they'd left the inn a few hours before. Rhys had ridden outside the entire time, as if he was just as dedicated to putting distance between them as she was. She ought to have been pleased at that thought, but instead she'd been restless. She had tried to read and couldn't concentrate. When Nan chatted with her, she found herself becoming distracted.

It would not do, especially since they were stopping for a picnic lunch before moving on for the day. She would have to sit beside Rhys again and pretend everything was fine.

The door opened on that thought, and the man himself peeked in. "Good afternoon, ladies," he said, calm and casual, as if he weren't troubled at all as she was.

And of course he likely wasn't. Every once in a while he looked at her like he felt a stirring of the same connection she did. Perhaps he found her attractive. But that didn't seem to make him uncomfortable. Likely it meant nothing to him.

"My lord," she said, and heard how cold her tone sounded.

He held out a hand to her, and she swallowed hard before she took it. Even though they were each wearing gloves, the spark from making contact with him still rippled through her. She released him as soon as she could, pacing toward the wide field where the driver and groom were spreading out the food packed back at the inn earlier in the day.

She drew a long breath of fresh air.

"Beautiful day, isn't it?" Rhys asked, motioning her toward the blanket.

She nodded. "We've been very lucky with the weather both days. So late in the summer, I might have expected rain."

They sat on the blanket and everyone began to eat. And though she had expected that she might have to make small talk with Rhys for the hour they paused in their travels, it turned out not to be true. Instead he chatted with the servants, asking after families and laughing at their jokes. She couldn't help but stare in wonder.

Men of Rhys's rank were not often so kind to those they considered beneath them. Growing up on the periphery of his world had shown her that over and over again. Servants were not thought of by many a man of title or money.

But this man was different, better in a thousand tiny ways. Kind and friendly, open to differing opinions, deferent to those who had more information or experience, even if they were not as elevated in stature. He apologized for his wrongs, he made amends for those that weren't even his.

And sitting there, watching him, she felt the stir of those emotions he inspired. Lust, yes. And that one she could have forgiven herself for. He was handsome, after all. Many a woman probably felt a tingling in her loins when he passed by.

The real trouble came from the deeper emotions she felt. Stirrings in her heart that made her want things she most certainly couldn't have. She and Rhys could be nothing more than acquaintances with a common goal to protect the child for whom they shared responsibility.

She blinked as she pushed to her feet.

"That was a lovely meal," she said. "I think I shall take a short walk, if that will not slow our progress. I'd like to stretch my legs."

"It will take us a moment to tidy up from lunch," Nan said.

"Aye, ma'am, and there will be chores to be done before we carry on the road," the driver added. "Take your time."

She nodded, cast one last furtive glance toward the man who inspired such tangled reactions in her and started across the green field. She tried to settle herself by grabbing onto the sensations around her. The way the tall reeds brushed her skirts, the smell of heather, the sound of chirping birds and, when she crested a small hill, the sight of a clear, blue lake reflecting the cloudless sky above.

Water had always been a soothing influence on her. She'd loved the sea the few times she'd been able to visit it. And while this tiny lake was certainly far from the sea, she still moved toward it, hoping the lapping of the small waves on the pebbled shore would help calm her riotous mind.

She reached the edge and stood there, staring out over the expanse. Yes, this was better. A few moments here would do the trick, and then she would be right as rain again.

Except she was not left alone. Behind her she heard a voice on the breeze.

"Phillipa?"

She turned back and found no one there, but after a brief moment Rhys appeared over the rise that blocked the view of the carriage a few hundred yards away. Her heart firmly lodged itself in her throat and she pursed her lips in disgust at how quickly she was back in this place of wicked longing.

"My lord," she said, and turned her back on him to stare at the lake again. "I did not realize you intended to join me."

He stopped beside her, at a reasonable distance, but still too close. She could smell the sandalwood goodness of his skin even now.

"I thought your idea of stretching your legs was a good one," he said. "This is lovely—I had no idea the lake was here or we might have had our picnic on the shore."

She grunted her response and refused to look in his direction. He was quiet a moment and then he turned to face her. "I didn't do something to…to offend you, did I?" he asked.

Her shoulders rolled forward. Blast and damn him, now he would make her feel guilty for being petulant when all he ever had been from the moment he met her was kind. Did he deserve that just because *she* couldn't control herself? Of course not.

She drew a long breath. "I apologize if you sensed a shift in my attitude. The closer we come to Bath, the more anxious I seem to become. There are many duties to face there. And memories, not all of them pleasant."

That was the partial truth, of course. He didn't need to know the rest. It would only complicate things.

He bent his head. "Of course."

"I hope you aren't expecting a magnificent estate to greet you," she said, worrying her hands in front of her, one over the other. "The home your brother purchased in Bath is not terrible by any means, but it isn't the finest, either. I have kept it as well as I could, but you will likely be able to hear Kenley if he stirs at night. It's…" She swallowed. "Close quarters."

His pupils dilated a fraction and his gaze swept over her entire body in one heated glance. Damn, she wished he wouldn't do that. It only made her legs clench, and she didn't want to clench her legs around this man.

"I hope I won't be intruding," he said, his voice a little rougher.

"Oh no, that wasn't what I meant," she began.

Now they were speaking at the same time. Him apologizing for not thinking and offering to stay elsewhere, her trying to back away from what she realized now had sounded rude.

He reached out and caught her hand, she thought to stay her words, and it worked. Not because he had comforted her, but because the sizzle of awareness silenced her. She stared down at her hand in his, then back up to his face.

"Phillipa," he said softly.

She squeezed her eyes shut. He always called her by her first name because having three Mrs. Montgomerys in the same household had been too confusing. But he had no idea what hearing her name from his lips did to her. There was something about how the sound rolled out in his voice, like a caress.

"Please don't," she whispered. She should have pulled her hand away, but she didn't.

There was a hesitation of just a beat, and then he asked, "Don't do what?"

She let her eyes open and found that he was staring at her intently now. The world faded in the blue of his eyes, and she caught her breath as she tried to find words. Thoughts. Anything at all.

"You must know what," she whispered. "You are a man of experience, a man of the world. You must know what you're doing right now."

He swallowed, that action working his throat even beneath the wrapping of his cravat. It felt like the moment stretched forever, and then he stepped closer and the distance was suddenly no longer appropriate.

"Phillipa," he whispered. She bent her head, but he caught her chin and gently tilted it back toward him. "Phillipa," he said again, but this time it didn't carry. It was just his lips moving to make the words.

"Please," she murmured, uncertain if she was begging for more or for him to be the one to rein in this madness.

He chose the former, and his dark head bent toward her. She met him halfway, her hands resting against his broad chest as he claimed her lips. It couldn't be called a kiss, which sounded sweet, chaste even. No, this was claiming. This was surrender to an animal desire that had been building for weeks. An inevitable capitulation to something they both knew was wrong. Both knew could never come to anything. They *could not* kiss.

But they *were* kissing and Phillipa was burning alive. She lifted against him, the sound of his name muffled on her tongue. His fingers flexed against her back, heated branding she wanted to last forever, to prove this had happened later when she tried to tell herself it was a dream. When he had left her life, never to return.

That thought jolted her from the madness a fraction. She realized they were standing out in the open, where anyone could stumble upon them. The last thing either one of them needed.

And so responsibility returned and she pulled back, her breath short as she stared up at him. For a moment, there was no clarity in his expression, only that animal hunger that had driven them to this in the first place. But slowly, he returned to himself.

And she saw the moment where reality dawned for him.

He backed away, far away, and stared at her. "Phillipa, I-I am so sorry. I don't know what came over me."

He wouldn't meet her eyes. He'd always done so in the past, but now he refused, and her stomach turned. This moment, so powerful and so wonderful...had ruined everything between them. She could see that it had. That he would pull further away because of his sense of duty, because of the weight pressing down on his shoulders.

Kissing her had made it worse, not better.

"Emotions h-have been...high lately," she stammered, searching for any explanation that would lower this wall he was clearly going to build between them. "And our friendship has become one I greatly value. This was a moment of weakness, of confusion. You needn't apologize for it. I was as swept away as you were."

"You are too kind," he said with a bow, suddenly all formality. "Though I don't deserve anything less than your censure. I assure you, this won't happen again."

The certainty of the words stung like he'd slapped her, and she turned her face so he wouldn't be aware of the tears that suddenly tingled in her eyes. He wasn't being unkind. He was being gentlemanly.

And yet he tore her heart out in ways that were too revealing, even to herself.

"I understand," she said, wishing her voice didn't have that slight waver to it.

"We should probably go back," he said, shifting with discomfort. "The others will be ready by now, I think."

"Of course," she said, and moved toward the safety of others over the rise. "I'm anxious to reach our destination."

He said nothing more, but followed her up the hill. She felt his eyes on her as they walked together across the field back toward the carriage. But he said nothing to her as she allowed the footman to help her into the rig for the final leg of their journey.

He said nothing, and that said it all.

R hys had never wanted his half-brother's things. All his life, it had been quite the opposite. While Erasmus was showy and bold, Rhys had been quiet, studious, careful. They'd never had the same taste in anything.

And now, as he rode along on this horse beside his carriage, winding down the miles taking him to Bath, all he could think about was how deeply he coveted Phillipa.

For hours he had only thought about the kiss. No, that wasn't true. He'd thought about the kiss a great deal, of course. How could one not when it had been such a magnificent explosion of mouths and tongues and gripping hands? The kind of kiss that made a man want to forget everything else in the world, something Rhys didn't often have occasion to do.

But he thought of more than that. He thought of all the places that kiss could have gone, there on the soft grass beside the lake. How if they'd been alone, if she hadn't pulled away, if…if…if…

Then he might have given in to this dissolute part of himself that he so wanted to hide. He might have taken far more than a stolen kiss.

When he was honest with himself, this wasn't the first time such fantasies had plagued his mind. Almost since the first moment he entered a room and Phillipa was there with her wild mop of curly hair and her bright green eyes with their flicker of defiance and self-assurance, he had wanted her. Deeply, desperately, wanted her. The kind of want that kept him awake at night, that woke him hard in the morning, that made him breathless when he saw her.

And it was fucking terrible. If he'd met her first, if there had been no Erasmus, it wouldn't have been. It would have been something wonderful then, perhaps. But there *was* an Erasmus. And a marriage. And a scandal.

So nothing good could ever come of any of this now. Phillipa was largest on a pile of things he could not have, should not want.

"There, my lord!" the driver said as they came to a rise in the road.

Rhys blinked, pulled from his thoughts, and looked down at the city below. Bath. A bustling resort town, with unique terraced houses and columned buildings and, of course, the famous Roman baths that brought so many there each year.

It didn't take them long to enter the outskirts of the city, where the bustle increased exponentially. Rhys had always liked the heartbeat of a city. He stayed in London rather than retreating to his country estate during holidays, so the bright, cheerful chaos of Bath was appealing. Although the happy faces of those walking the streets, enjoying their holidays, were almost an insult to the weight he carried.

He frowned and glanced at the carriage. He could see Phillipa's face in the window. She had pushed the curtain back and was staring intently at the scene around them. Her lips were pursed, her expression lined with concern. Then her gaze slid to him and her eyes widened a fraction. Her mouth parted. The curtain fell and she leaned away back into the carriage.

He frowned as he returned his attention to the road ahead of him. He deserved the distancing Phillipa had just done. It was exactly what he'd demanded by the lake after their kiss. It was what they both needed in order to move forward with the complicated lives stretched out before them.

But he didn't like it.

They weaved their way out of the town proper and into the more sparsely populated areas on the fringes. At last the carriage turned down a short drive and finally stopped in front of a cottage pushed back from the road. A shrubbery-lined pathway led to the door, and as he slung himself off his horse, it opened.

Two people exited, and older man and woman, and in her arms was a chubby, smiling baby. This was his nephew, the child his brother had abandoned.

In that moment, as Rhys looked at the boy, something in him shifted. It was like the air had been yanked from his lungs and he couldn't look away as the boy was brought closer. His heart raced, swelling with emotions he had never thought to have for a child.

In that moment, Rhys knew he would do everything in his power to make sure the boy never knew grief, never knew loneliness, never wanted for anything.

No matter the cost.

CHAPTER 5

Pippa nearly deposited herself on her backside, she exited the carriage so swiftly. But what did a lack of decorum matter when Kenley was right there, just a few feet away? She pushed forward, past Rhys who was standing stock still at the end of the path and raced toward him.

It had been weeks since she saw the baby, but his eyes lit up as she neared and he reached for her, chubby arms flexing as he gurgled his excitement.

She swept him from Mrs. Barton's arms and cuddled him close, speaking nonsense to him as she drew in deep whiffs of his soft baby scent. God, they could bottle it and she would make a mint.

"He's so big!" she declared with a smile for Mr. and Mrs. Barton, for her butler was the husband of the housekeeper. Two kinder people she never could have met. "Good day to you both."

They returned the greeting, though she was aware of how their gazes both shifted to the man behind her. Not that she could blame them. Lord Leighton was now their employer and they did not know him. They didn't know they had nothing to fear.

"Lord Leighton, may I present Mr. and Mrs. Barton," she said, turning toward Rhys. He was staring at Kenley, not the servants, and she could not read his expression. "My butler...though to be fair, Mr. Barton has always been far more than that. He is a man of all trades and I could not do without him. And Mrs. Barton, my housekeeper. They have very kindly watched your nephew during my absence."

Rhys blinked, and it was as if he'd been brought back to reality. "Good day," he mumbled. "Very pleased to make your acquaintance."

"My lord," Mr. Barton said, and Mrs. Barton curtseyed slightly as a greeting.

Which left only one final duty. She moved a little closer to Rhys and smiled, hoping she could encourage him when it came to the child. "And this is your nephew, my lord. Kenley Montgomery."

Rhys's hand flexed at his side and trembled as he gently reached toward Kenley. Kenley tracked it, but when Rhys was about to touch him, the baby cowered a little, putting his head into Pippa's shoulder to look at his uncle shyly.

She laughed as she cuddled him a bit for comfort, but her smile fell as she saw Rhys's forlorn expression. "He does not like me," he said.

She shook her head. "He doesn't know you. Most children are a bit shy of strangers, but I assure you that within the day he'll likely warm to you. And then you will not be able to make him stop reaching for you."

A flutter of a smile touched Rhys's lips, but then it faded as he stared again at Kenley.

"You two must be tired from the long journey," Mrs. Barton said, breaking the spell that had spun up around them and Kenley. "Come inside, won't you? We have a lovely tea ready and the chambers are prepared if you need a rest."

Pippa turned back to her servants and smiled. "That sounds divine. I cannot wait. I have dreamed of your raspberry tarts for weeks, Mrs. Barton. Please tell me they're on the menu."

"Made fresh this morning, just for you, Mrs. Montgomery," Mrs. Barton said, and then gasped. "Or...should I...what might I..."

Pippa blushed. She knew the scandal about Erasmus's multiple wives had circulated through all of Society. She'd never had any illusion otherwise. But now she had to face it, from two people she cared for, and it stung in a new way.

"Mrs. Montgomery is fine," she said. "It is too difficult to think of another way to do this."

"Very good," Mrs. Barton said. "Would you like me to take the baby while you eat?"

"No," Pippa said, and snuggled him closer. He'd begun to tug her curls and she had forgotten how much she loved that little habit of his. "I could not put him down for all the raspberry tarts in England!"

They entered the cottage, and she did her best not to look at Rhys. He was so accustomed to finer things—she almost didn't want to know what he thought of her simple home. He said nothing, of course. He was too gentlemanly and simply followed them to the parlor where the tea was arranged.

They sat and she shifted Kenley to one knee as Mrs. Barton bustled to serve them.

"I swear, he has grown so much in such a short time," Pippa breathed as she pinched his cheek lightly and elicited a giggle that warmed her heart. "Tell me everything he did while we were apart."

Mrs. Barton recited all the things Kenley had done, including sitting up on his own.

"Oh, and I missed it!" Pippa declared with a frown.

"He'll certainly do it again," Mrs. Barton said with a laugh. "Is there anything else you might need?"

Pippa glanced at Rhys, but he was staring at his plate, seemingly in some other world. She frowned. "No, I think we're fine. I know Kenley's nap is soon, I promise I'll surrender him when the time comes."

Mrs. Barton laughed and slipped from the room, leaving Pippa alone with Rhys and Kenley. She picked at the tart she had been so excited about and watched him.

"You must have questions," she said softly.

He lifted his gaze to her. "I hardly know where to start."

She nodded. "It's overwhelming, I'm sure. The idea of a baby is one thing, the reality something else entirely. Shall I tell you about him?"

"Please."

"He is nine months old," she began. "He was born in early December of last year. He's been a very healthy child and seems to be growing at a normal rate. He likes birds a great deal and tracks them when he sees them." She smiled. "Mr. Barton bought him the sweetest little wooden bird toy."

"Mr. Barton," Rhys said softly. "Not his father."

She cleared her throat and gave Kenley a small piece of tart, which cause a drooling display of joy that lightened the mood. At least for her.

"His father never claimed him," she said softly. "At least not in public."

Rhys pushed back from the table with a screech of chair legs that made Kenley jolt in her arms. "I...I think I am overly tired. Perhaps I should rest before I consider these facts, before I decide what I should do. I..." He looked at her, looked at Kenley. "I am sorry, Phillipa."

She opened her mouth to speak, but he ignored her and stalked from the room. She stared after him, eyes stinging with tears for the obvious struggle he was having. What would it mean for Kenley? Rhys had always been decent and kind in the dealings she had with him, but she had watched men of title for many years. She knew that some flinched when they were made uncomfortable. Backed away.

And that could leave Kenley penniless and without important friends to protect him both from the more undefined dangers and the ones that were very real. His mother, for instance, had disappeared after murdering his father. What if she returned? What would it mean for him then?

She shivered as Mrs. Barton entered the room. "It's time for Master Kenley to take his afternoon rest. Oh, I didn't realize Lord Leighton had left you."

Pippa pursed her lips. "I think Lord Leighton is slightly overwhelmed."

"Don't know how he couldn't be, poor man. Nor you, ma'am. We have thought of you often and I hope that you are well through all this...turmoil."

Pippa bent her head. "All the worst news reached you, I suppose."

Mrs. Barton shrugged as she took Kenley. "I know better than to believe gossip spun up as fact. Forgive me for saying, but you look tired, yourself, Mrs. Montgomery. Perhaps you should follow Lord Leighton's lead and rest yourself the remainder of the day."

"Perhaps you're right," Pippa said with a warm smile for the kind woman.

She kissed Kenley and watched as Mrs. Barton took him away for his nap. But the moment they were gone, she took three big bites of her much-desired tart for courage, set her napkin aside and got to her feet.

She wanted to rest. She felt tired to her bones after everything that had turned her world upside down in the past few weeks... months...years. But she didn't have that luxury, not when she had responsibilities to the child she'd just been holding. She owed him her full attention until she was certain of his future.

Which meant she forced herself to stride from the parlor and down the hallway. She wasn't certain where Rhys had gone. His bedchamber was a logical choice, and if he had gone there, she would follow and barge into his private space. But she avoided thinking of that. Thinking about it felt very dangerous.

Luckily, she didn't have to go upstairs and rattle his doors. When she paused to peek into Erasmus's small study, she found Rhys there, standing beside the window, looking down onto the street. She felt the tension in him even from this distance. She felt the anguish and it touched her far more than it should have.

She stepped into the room and silently shut the door behind her. She drew a few long breaths before she turned back. He was still staring out at the street and she cleared her throat softly. "My lord?"

He jumped at the sound of her voice and pivoted to face her. She caught her breath at his expression. He looked drawn down to nothing in the sunshine coming through the window and hiding nothing from her. Like he could cry or break everything in this room. Like he could collapse into a heap under the weight of everything he had to carry thanks to his feckless, foolish brother. One she recognized he'd had no time to mourn.

Rhys looked broken, and in that charged moment she wanted so badly to fix things for him.

She crossed the room toward him. He tracked her, those blue eyes taking in everything, but he didn't back away. That was something, at any rate. She caught his hand and held it between her own.

"Oh, please," she said. "Please talk to me."

His body gave a great twitch, and he turned his head so he was no longer looking at her. "Perhaps that is not a good idea," he said, his voice rough. "Considering the kiss and our mutual vow to maintain distance."

The rejection stung, and she wanted to let him turn away. But in the end that would only protect herself, not Kenley. Not Rhys. So she drew in a breath and squeezed his hand a little tighter. The action forced him to look down at her again. Drown her in those beautiful blue eyes.

"Of course you're right," she began, voice trembling like her entire body was trembling. "But my lord...Rhys...we are the only two in this world in the middle of this. The only ones who can fully understand each other. You came here to help me, I want to help you."

She leaned a little closer, even though it was too close. She could feel the warmth of his breath stir her skin, feel the shift in him that told her she wasn't the only one haunted by that kiss. "Please let me. Please."

R hys felt the weight of Phillipa's hands around his, the warmth of her body seeping through his bloodstream. He caught every hitch in her breath and tremble of her body. All of it consumed him and made it hard to think, let alone speak.

But she had made a good point. In this horrible destruction, they were two of the few survivors. The only two in this house. And if they didn't lean on each other, there would be no one else who understood.

"He looks like my brother," he choked out.

She bent her head. "Kenley," she whispered.

He nodded. "Who in turn looked like our father, far more than I ever did."

"That's how I determined the child's parentage, you know," she admitted, and her cheeks flamed the most fetching pink, though he hated the reason for it.

"How did that happen?" he asked. "All of this is so convoluted, between a fake murder and a real murder and a woman with two names and a child he didn't claim."

She choked out a humorless laugh. "Perhaps we should sit before the fire if I'm to tell this tale."

"I'll pour some whisky," he suggested, and went to the sideboard to pour them each one. When he returned, she took hers and slung back half of it in one gasping sip. "That bad?" he asked as he sat.

She met his gaze. "Very much so." She cleared her throat as she fiddled with the lip of her glass, tracing it with her fingertip. "When we married, Erasmus did not wish for me to bring along my maid to our new home. I'd known her for years and I argued it strenuously, but he insisted, over and over, and finally I relented."

"What reason could he have possibly had?" Rhys asked.

She shrugged. "Any reason he thought would sway me. He said he wished to start our life fresh in a new house with new servants, he said she was untrustworthy, he said she had stared at him too long."

Rhys pursed his lips as he tried to rein in his anger at this topic. "He was always very good at demanding his own way."

"Given the story you told me last night during supper, it seems he was taught that he could," she said.

He bent his head. He didn't regret giving her that glimpse into his soul, but it was odd to have someone know so much of his past that he had generally kept hidden. But here they were.

"Yes," he agreed.

She shook her head as if trying to refocus. "Once we moved here, he told me he had hired a new maid for me. I was shocked. I'd been given no ability to interview this woman myself, I hadn't been asked for my needs or preferences." She drew in a long breath. "It was the first time I had an inkling he didn't care about them at all. I shoved that feeling aside, though. I forced myself to keep believing I'd made the right choice in him."

Rhys pursed his lips. It was such an odd thing to think this woman he craved so deeply had once been his brother's wife, even if not legally. He couldn't picture them together. In truth, he didn't want to.

"He brought this woman in, and she was very pretty, very young. Dark haired and eyed. Of course I had no idea that she was Erasmus's first love, his true love, Rosie Stanton. He called her Rachel, I suppose to cover up the truth in case I dug for it."

"How did she behave toward you?" Rhys asked.

"Cool. Mostly professional, though I think she purposefully pinched me helping me into my clothes and often tugged hard combing my hair." She shrugged. "I suppose it was her only recourse against a woman who was leading the life she thought she deserved. Six months into the marriage, he started acting more...cool... toward me. Some nights he wouldn't come home, or at least he wouldn't come to our chamber. And nine months into the marriage, Rosie came to me and told me she was..."

She broke off, and in that moment Rhys saw the pain etched across her face, the humiliation that she normally seemed capable of shrugging off like it meant nothing. Phillipa used her strength as a shield, easily pretending that nothing had ever hurt her.

But so much had. Beneath the armor were so many scars. And he ached for them and for her.

"She was with child," he finished for her.

"Yes." Her voice trembled and she finished the rest of her whisky with as big of a swig as the first one. "With my husband's child. And I was too stupid to realize it."

CHAPTER 6

Nausea hit Pippa in waves, and she wished she hadn't wolfed down half a tart and an entire tumbler of whisky in rapid succession. She had never spoken about any of this to any other person. Mr. and Mrs. Barton had pieced it together themselves and were too polite to mention it. Too kind.

Once she arrived in London and met Abigail and Celeste, she'd thought of sharing the truth then. The two women had become her confidantes in a great many things. But up until the bitter end, she hadn't shared Kenley's existence with the other two Mrs. Montgomerys. They had only found out when they'd all nearly been killed by Erasmus and Rosie.

She'd told herself that was to protect the child. But in truth, this was her private pain. Her private humiliation.

Yet when Rhys asked, she'd handed it over to him, tied with an ugly ribbon. Now he held it, watching her as he digested it. She wished she could read his expression. Wished she understood the workings of his mind.

She cleared her throat and continued, "When Rosie told me she was with child and that the man responsible had vanished from her life, I felt terrible for her."

She broke off because it felt like her throat was closing. Now Rhys's expression softened and he shifted in his chair as if he wanted to reach for her. "Phillipa."

She lifted a hand. If he touched her right now, she feared she'd shatter. "I can do this. I can say it." She drew a few breaths and then carried on as best she could. "A mistake of that magnitude could destroy a woman, and I didn't want to see Rosie damaged. How the two of them must have laughed when I insisted we allow her to stay on. Erasmus even made a show of disagreeing, of making me fight for it before he relented."

"Manipulative prick," Rhys muttered, and his cheeks flamed with anger.

She shrugged. "In hindsight I can see that. I can understand that it was all part of their wicked plan."

"And was he still outwardly disagreeable to her as her confinement continued?"

She pushed to her feet and worried her hands as she paced the small room. "Oh no. On the contrary, the moment I walked into their trap, he changed his tune. He told me she ought not to do her maid duties while she was increasing."

"He hired another maid?"

"No." She choked on a laugh. "Nor would he allow me to. It was fine, I knew how to take care of myself. He also insisted we make Rosie comfortable. Suddenly her room was filled with fine things, only the best. I was so blind that I thought he was merely a decent man acting decently."

"Did you ever confront him on his sudden attentiveness?" he asked.

"Once. A few months in, he began pondering names for her child. He'd do it out loud at the supper table. I asked him why he was so involved in her life, with her confinement. And he laughed. He *laughed* and told me I had insisted she stay. That this was my fault."

Rhys's nostrils flared, but he said nothing. She sighed. "After that, I ignored it when I caught them with their heads together, when I saw the little looks between them. I even pretended it away when she touched her belly and asked me if I'd ever wanted a child. She was...*mocking* me. I lay in my bed and stared at my ceiling and knew it, but I did nothing and I said nothing. What you must think of me."

He did get up now and crossed to her in two long strides. Now it was he who caught her hands, just as she had done to him when she followed him here. Rhys's gaze bore into hers, filled with fire and understanding all at once.

"I think you are a good woman who was taken advantage of by two wicked people bent on only their own desires," he said. "You weren't foolish, you were manipulated by my brother and his lover. And having been at the sharp end of his manipulations in the past, I can tell you there was no one better at them. He could confuse your own memory, convince you that your name wasn't what you thought. When he wanted something, he was ruthless. He was ruthless with you, Phillipa. He was cruel and thoughtless and that *isn't* your fault."

He said that with such certainty, such conviction, that for a brief moment she believed him. After months of torturing herself, it was freeing to believe she hadn't been at fault for her blindness. And oh, how she wanted to step closer to him. To let his arms come around her like they had at the shore of the lake earlier in the day.

She wanted everything she couldn't have and more.

Which was why she stepped away. "Thank you," she whispered.

There was a long, heavy silence between them, and then Rhys asked, "How long after the boy was born did you know?"

"Well, at first he just looked like a baby," she said. "I noted that he had blue eyes, but I told myself lots of people have blue eyes, not just Erasmus."

"My eyes too," Rhys said.

She wrinkled her brow and looked at him closer. "They're the same color," she said slowly, examining that remarkable sea blue.

"But they *aren't* the same as his. Yours are...warm. Kind. I never look at them and see him. Never."

There was a palpable relief that washed over him with that statement. As if having the same eyes as his wicked brother was deeply troubling, or that her seeing them as the same was. But what she'd said was true. She'd never seen them as equal.

"It wasn't the eyes, anyway," she said. "It should have been, perhaps, but it was that as Kenley got older, he started to have his father's nose. He started to turn his head like Erasmus...you know that little side tilt—"

Rhys nodded. "I know the one. When he was thinking of something, trying to find an answer...or a lie."

"Well, Kenley does that too. And I just...knew."

"You confronted my brother and Rosie," he said.

"Erasmus was long gone by then, rushed off to the next wife and the stalking of the next after that." She shivered. "I couldn't confront him, so instead I went to Rosie. She didn't even try to lie. She just laughed in my face. And the next day she disappeared, abandoning the child to, as we now know, join Erasmus in London and assist him in his ultimate plan to fake his own death, have Abigail blamed for it and let Rosie collect the payoff he thought you'd give Kenley."

"But you didn't know any of that."

"Of course not." She threw up her hands. "I thought he was a philanderer who had impregnated my maid and was now shirking his duties. I was incensed he could do that to a child I already cared deeply for. I wanted him to assure Kenley's future, to admit that he owed the baby a debt as his father, even if he would never allow the boy to have his name. I started trying to find him, writing him, and that's how I ended up going to London."

Rhys was staring at her now, expression filled with a wonder that made her shift in discomfort. "What is that...why are you looking at me that way?" she asked.

"You put all your energy and time, all your emotion, into

protecting a child who was living proof of a betrayal. Of the end of a marriage. That is...not everyone would do that, Phillipa."

She shrugged. "I love Kenley. I couldn't love him more if he were mine. I grew close to him when Rosie was still my maid, and when she left, I knew he was my responsibility. I wouldn't have wanted it any other way." She bent her head. "And Kenley wasn't the end of my marriage."

Rhys stepped a little closer. "No?"

She shrugged. "I had convinced myself I cared for Erasmus at the start. And I didn't hate being his wife for a while. But I'd realized around the same time that he was impregnating his lover that I'd made a mistake. I'd realized he wasn't the man I thought him to be, nor the one I wanted him to be. And he didn't care enough to change." She lifted her hands in surrender. "And now, of course, I see the full breadth of why. I was just a tool, a weapon that provided him with more money and more time in his schemes."

"Again, his failing, not yours," Rhys said.

"Isn't it?" she whispered.

He was close enough to touch her, and she knew he would even before he did. His fingers traced her jawline, almost a feather-light stroke. As if he made it soft enough they could pretend it wasn't happening. That the line wasn't being crossed.

"You *never* failed," he said. "He was a fool not to look at you and worship you and fight to keep you at his side. An utter and complete fool."

His head dipped as he said the words, and she lifted into him even though she knew she shouldn't. Their mouths met, this time gently rather than with animal passion as they had earlier in the day. He brushed his mouth back and forth over hers as his fingers curled around her biceps and he tugged her just a little closer still.

She heard herself moan. A soft sound of surrender and she parted her lips slightly. Now it was he who groaned in response and his tongue edged past the barrier. She reveled in the taste of him, in the warmth of him, in the way that just this stolen touch woke sensations in her that she hadn't ever felt before. Made her want things she'd never fully understood. He was a brave new world, she wanted to explore every inch of it without fear.

But he wouldn't allow it. Just as he had by the lake, he caught his breath and stepped away. He released her, dragging a hand through his hair as he pivoted to walk to the fire, his shoulders lifting with panting.

"You are right that we are the only two who understand this situation," he gasped out. "And if we...blur those lines..." He faced her and shook his head. "I don't want confusion to cause pain, Phillipa. You have suffered more than enough of that these last few months...years."

Embarrassment wracked her, though he hadn't been anything but kind in his rejection. Both times.

"O-of course," she replied, hating herself for the stammer that revealed too much. "We are both overwrought, both overwhelmed. This will not happen again, my lord. I'll leave you."

She moved to do just that, but he stepped toward her. "Phillipa."

She stopped, gripping her hands at her sides as she waited for whatever he would say next. "Yes?"

"I do wish to be your friend," he said. "You have called me Rhys a handful of times, and I'd like for you to continue to do so."

This was an olive branch. Some kind of way for her to see that he didn't judge her as harshly as she judged herself. A kindness offered and yet it stung.

"You already call me Phillipa thanks to the fact that there were three Mrs. Montgomerys in London," she said. "I'm fine if you continue calling me that."

"Not Pippa?" he asked.

She bit her lip. Her friends called her Pippa, that was true. She thought of herself the same way. And yet she *liked* the way he said her full name. She liked that he was the only one who did that. She liked the way it made her legs clench and her breath catch.

"The longer name, the more formal name...perhaps it helps us keep up those lines that we cannot cross," she said. Lied. She lied. "And now I will find Mr. Barton and have him show you to your chamber. A rest will do us both good and clear our heads for all the decisions that must be made regarding the future." She shook her head. "Kenley's future. That is the most important thing now."

She left the room without waiting for his response. She didn't want whatever he said to distract her from that declaration that put the stakes in terms she couldn't forget. Whatever her desire for the man in the room behind her, her duty was to a child who could not advocate for himself.

And she could never ignore that.

CHAPTER 7

Pippa woke early, as she always did. Even when she regularly attended her father's assembly until the wee hours, she'd still woken with the sun. She liked being the first one awake in the quiet, able to think without interruptions or distractions.

Last night, of course, she had not attended an assembly. She'd been here in her little house, tucked in and quiet after a delicious supper. The only thing different about this night than a dozen nights before it was that Rhys had been sitting across her at that supper, and in the parlor afterward.

It had all been extremely appropriate, of course. After that last kiss in the study, he had been nothing but proper. Formal, even. They had discussed Kenley's day-to-day schedule, the weather, a book they'd both enjoyed.

It all felt like tension. Like putting up blinders to what was happening beneath the surface. But this was how it had to be, so surrendering to it was exactly what had to happen.

Now, though, as she roamed the quiet halls of the small house, she tried not to let her mind wander to darker thoughts. Deeper needs and wants. To dreams about Rhys that she could not seem to control.

"Good morning, Mrs. Montgomery."

She jumped and turned to face Mrs. Barton, who had stepped from the breakfast room to greet her. "Good morning," she said, and was glad her tone sounded normal when her heart was racing.

"I hope you slept well," Mrs. Barton said. "Will you need anything this morning?"

"Oh, no. You and Mr. Barton take care of your duties, I'm fine. I'm going to Mr. Montgomery's study." As Mrs. Barton's face fell, Pippa shrugged. "We have to go through his things at some point. The future will come—we must be prepared for it."

Mrs. Barton worried her hands before her. "Do you have any idea what we can expect of that future? What Lord Leighton has in mind?"

Pippa hesitated. "We have not yet had a long discussion on that topic," she admitted. "But I can tell you that his lordship is a man who can be trusted. I believe he acts in good faith, toward all of us. But I know the uncertainty is uneasy, so I will inform you as soon as I have further news."

"Yes, ma'am," Mrs. Barton said. "Very good."

The housekeeper gave a nod as Pippa headed up the hall to the study. As she entered, she let her breath out in a long sigh. She'd seen the hesitation on her housekeeper's face. Mrs. Barton had doubted her when she spoke of Rhys's character.

And why not? After all, she had once believed in Erasmus.

"But it wasn't the same," she whispered. And that was true. Her connection with Erasmus had always been built on...uncertainty. She'd thought him a free spirit. He'd show up when he pleased, surprise her with gifts or expectations that she would drop everything to do as he desired. Even after their marriage, she'd never fully been able to get a handle on who and what he was.

Much to her own detriment in the end.

But Rhys was different. No brothers could have been so opposite. Where Erasmus was scattered, Rhys was steady. He was calm in the storm—he wasn't the storm, itself. The only place that seemed untrue was when he touched her.

She glanced at the spot in the room where he had kissed her the previous afternoon. She recalled that rumble of his chest as he took her mouth, the tension that seemed to flow through every muscle of his body. *Then* she felt the danger beneath the surface. The barely contained power of his desire.

And foolishly she wanted it, despite having suffered for such things in the past.

She blinked and tried to clear her head. She hadn't come here to moon over Rhys or dissect the lesser points of her marriage. She had work to do and she was going to do it.

She sat in the chair behind the desk. Erasmus hadn't liked her in this room during their ill-fated union. When he was out of town, he locked it and took the only key with him. She'd had Mr. Barton break the lock in order to get in before she left for London, when she was trying to find Erasmus to confront him.

The seat was uncomfortable. Too hard, like the cushion hadn't been often used so it was never broken in. It seemed a room meant for work was only for show for Erasmus. Just like everything else in his life was for show.

She shook her head as she yanked open the top drawer of the desk. It was full of papers and tangled ribbons and dust. She'd dug through the items there looking for an address weeks and weeks ago, but never looked deeper. Now her heart throbbed as she stared at the messy pile.

Before she could get too far, the door to the study opened. She looked up, expecting Mrs. Barton to be there with a cup of tea, but instead it was Rhys who now stood in the entryway. He stared at her and she at him before she forced herself to her feet.

"G-Good morning," she stammered. Oh, why couldn't he be less attractive to her? Why couldn't this be easy?

"Phillipa," he said, his voice rough. "It seems we had the same thought."

"Yes," she said. "I suppose we must have. Though I admit I'm surprised to see you up so early."

He pursed his lips. "I've never been interested in the life of a layabout." He stepped into the room and looked around. His eyes lingered on the same place hers had a short time before. The place before the fire where they'd kissed.

Then he moved his gaze to her.

"I hope you know you don't have to do this," he said.

"Do what?" she asked.

"Go through his desk," he explained. "I imagine there might be... hurtful items to be found there."

She glanced down at the open drawer. "Yes, I'm sure there will be harmful things. But I must be a part of the search. After all, this is my house." She lifted her gaze back to his and the way he pursed his lips made her heart rate increase. "Isn't it?"

He sighed and reached back to close the door. She knew it was for privacy when it came to the delicate topic, but she still tracked the movement as if it could mean so much more.

Rhys stepped closer. "After Erasmus's death, in the weeks before we left London, I met with a solicitor in regards to his affairs."

"Please don't draw this out," she whispered. "Your expression is so frightening right now."

He shook his head. "I'm sorry. My brother made no arrangements...for any of his wives."

"Oh," she murmured as she collapsed back in the chair she had vacated. She set her hands on the desktop, staring at them as if they were attached to someone else.

Rhys edged closer. "All his assets, such that they are, seem to be returning to the estate. To me. Along with his not insignificant debts."

She managed to look up at him. "So it is as I guessed...the house here is yours," she said.

"It appears to be. Though I believe he might have taken loans out against it, so there are a few creditors who might make a claim."

"Oh God," she said, and rested her head down on her hands. Nausea washed over her and she sat there trying not to vomit for a moment.

But then, as the sick feeling faded, it was replaced by something else entirely. Anger. She'd so often felt that emotion when it came to Erasmus, but she'd always shoved it down, hoping to maintain some control over herself.

But now there was none of that. The rage rushed up in her, making her arms tingle, making her face hot as she lifted it to stare at Rhys.

"How could he?" she snapped. "How could he be so horrible, so selfish, so utterly graceless and cruel?"

She slammed her hands down against the desk. She hit it so hard, both her arms stung, and she shook her hands out as she got up and paced across the room. "That bastard took everything from anyone he encountered. From my friends, from his child. From me. He took my dignity, my future, my hopes."

She wiped at tears that had begun to burn her cheeks and tried to calm her breath, but it didn't seem possible.

Rhys was staring at her from across the room, and for a moment she thought he might chastise her for this unseemly display. But instead, he crossed the room. "Don't stop there. What else?"

"What?"

"What else, Phillipa? Say it all, don't let it fester inside of you." He caught her hands. "Say it."

"I hate him," she said. "I hate him so very much. I'm glad he is dead. I'm glad he can't ever hurt me or you again."

She tugged her hands away and clapped them both over her mouth as she stared at him. "Oh, Rhys, I'm sorry," she said through the web of her fingers. "I should not have said that."

His jaw set. "Some days I'm glad he is dead, too," he admitted softly. "You told me yesterday afternoon that we were both overwrought, overwhelmed, and I know that is true. I have an idea on how we could vent some of that emotion. Would you like to try?"

She felt the heat filling her cheeks at the suggestion. After all, she could think of a way to vent her emotions, too, but that couldn't be his proposal.

"I-I don't know," she said.

He smiled at her, and for a moment she was lost in the expression. He had so rarely smiled in the horrific weeks they'd known each other. But it was beautiful, like someone had pulled back the curtains in a dark room and revealed the most glorious summer day.

"Trust me," he said as he caught her hand and drew her toward the door. "I won't steer you wrong."

The fact that what he was about to do was highly inappropriate and ill-advised was something Rhys was trying not to focus on as he gathered a few items from his chamber before he rejoined Phillipa on the terrace where he'd left her moments before.

He had vowed to stay clear of her, especially in situations where they would be alone or too close. The temptation of her was far too great. And yet here he was, about to do both.

But what other choice did he have? She'd been so upset in the study. The anger he'd sometimes sensed just below the surface was bubbled up and the pain was almost palpable.

He wanted to help her. To somehow repair even a tiny fraction of the damage his wayward brother had done. And the best way to do that was to let her feel it. Stifling it was hurting her, so she had to let it out.

He hurried down the stairs and through the back of the house out onto the small terrace that overlooked a tidy garden. Phillipa stood across the expanse and turned to face him as he exited the house to join her.

His breath caught as he looked at her, just as it always did. She had calmed herself a little since her outburst, but her cheeks were still flushed with color, her blond curls bobbing around her face as if to frame that perfection. Taunt him with it.

She clenched her hands at her sides. "You brought a...a pillow?"

He glanced down at the pillow he'd taken from his bed. "Yes," he said. "And two cravats."

She blinked and her brow wrinkled with confusion. "I'm sorry, what are you having me do?"

"You'll see," he promised, and beckoned her closer by crooking his finger. She stared for a moment and then obeyed, and his cock made itself very known in that moment.

Christ, he was going to make things worse, not better, if he couldn't rein in his lust. He thought the least erotic thoughts he could as she reached him and tilted her head in question.

"Hold out your hand," he said. "Palm down."

She did so after a brief hesitation and he went to work wrapping it with the cravat. In and out, with expert skill, until he tied off the fabric and left her hand half-covered in silk.

"What are you doing?" she asked, but didn't resist when he grabbed the opposite hand and repeated the action there.

He focused on the work as best he could, rather than how soft her palm was, how her fingers curled against his as he worked the fabric in between each one.

"We are going to box," he said, and backed away from her.

She stared at him as if he'd suggested they swim out to sea and live in a fairyland island. "Box?" she repeated.

"It is a wonderful way to relieve strain," he said. "I go to my club in London regularly to punch through whatever is troubling me."

"Are you any good?" she asked.

He arched a brow. "The very best." Then he laughed. "That isn't true. I am middling, at most. I couldn't compete, if that's what you mean. But I don't have to be the best to enjoy something."

She smiled. "It isn't ladylike."

He arched a brow. "I will have you know that I've heard of a ladies club in London."

Her eyes went wide, though he thought he saw a flicker of interest in the green depths. "I cannot imagine."

"Now, in my club, we might have pads to hit, bags when we practice." He held up the pillow. "But this will have to do."

She seemed to ponder that a moment, perhaps letting what felt so foreign to her sink in. "So you want me to punch your pillow?"

He lowered it. "You'd prefer to punch me?"

She looked at the face in question. "Er, no. I like your face as it is."

"The highest compliment." He raised the pillow again. "Just swing. Don't think about form or anything else. Just hit the pillow."

She hesitated a moment, then cocked her fist back and grazed the pillow with it. He frowned as he dropped the pillow down. "That's the best you can do? After your display of anger in the study? Come, pretend the pillow is Erasmus."

Her lips parted. "I couldn't—"

"You can," he corrected her. "And, in fact, I insist you do."

She rolled her eyes like he was being ridiculous, but edged her way back. This time when she walloped the pillow, it was much harder. She hit it again, again, and the longer she hit, the more focused she became. She hit with one fist, then the other, over and over. She hit so hard she began to grunt with the exertion, that a thin sheen of sweat broke on her brow.

And with that exertion came emotion. Just like in the study, he could see her losing that firm grip she kept on her feelings. He could see the edges of her pain and her fear. Tears filled her eyes and then slid down her cheeks, and she just kept punching, wild and unkempt and beautiful now that she'd let it all go and was allowing herself to just *feel*.

She staggered with the last punch and tipped forward. He caught her as he dropped the pillow away and drew her against his chest. She wept there, great heaving gasps of sobs, her fingers clenching against his chest as she released everything she'd been holding inside.

"He shouldn't have done that to me," she gasped against his coat. "He shouldn't have done that to Kenley. He shouldn't have done that to you."

She lifted her face toward his and her eyes went wide. Her wrapped hand lifted and wiped his face, and only in that moment did he realize he was weeping too. For the same reasons, for different ones. For loss and unfairness and everything he'd wanted and could never have.

He lowered his head and their foreheads met gently. She caught his hands, her fingers tangling with his. And slowly, their panting breaths slowed to something deeper, something matched. Calm descended on him, nothing like he'd ever felt before, certainly nothing like what he'd felt in the last few months.

Despite the flurry of her emotion, she brought calm to him. And of how he wanted more of that. More of her. More of this one thing he definitely couldn't pursue.

"Phillipa," he whispered.

He had no idea what he would say to her. What he would ask. He never had a chance to find out because just as he was about to continue, the door to the terrace opened.

They stepped away. He pivoted toward the garden, pacing away from her as she turned to her butler, who was staring out at them with wide eyes. "Yes, Mr. Barton?"

"Master Kenley is up, Mrs. Montgomery," he said. "Mrs. Barton said you'd wanted to know."

"I did, thank you. Have her bring him to the breakfast room and I will join them there in a moment," she said.

The butler bowed his head and left them alone again on the terrace. Rhys forced himself to face her, uncertain what they should say or do. She smiled, something a little awkward but not untrue, and began to unwind his cravats from her hands. It was mesmerizing watching that swatch of cloth he wore against his throat come off her skin.

"Thank you," she whispered as she handed them back and motioned to the door. "We should go back in."

He nodded as he followed her through the hall. When they reached the breakfast room, he stopped, catching her elbow before she could leave him. She sucked in her breath when he touched her, just the slightest reaction, but he felt it down to his bones.

"I will arrange things for you, Phillipa. For him," he swore, holding her gaze so she would know he meant those words. "Nothing will be taken from you." He hesitated because certainly she had lost more than a good deal already. "Nothing more."

She bent her head. "I know."

They entered the breakfast room. Mrs. Barton was standing at the mirror above the mantel with Kenley. They turned as Phillipa entered, and Kenley's entire face lit up. So did Phillipa's. Rhys saw how closely connected they were, how special and strong their bond was.

And he knew, deep in his heart, deeper than his heart, that he had to keep the promise he had just made to this woman. He had to do everything in his power to make her happy. It was, perhaps, what he had been put on this earth to do.

CHAPTER 8

Phillipa sat on the floor in the parlor, watching as Kenley played with his blocks. "That's a square," she said as he lifted one of the smooth wooden toys toward her. "Square."

Kenley babbled empty noises as he slammed one block against the other and then rolled the one in his hand across the carpet.

She sighed and worried her lip. It had been three days since Rhys had taken her out on the terrace and let her vent her emotions. Three days since he'd touched her and held her and cried with her. He'd been busy since then, working away in Erasmus's study, going out into Bath where she thought he might have hired a solicitor to help him with the particulars.

She, however, was kept out of them. Rhys spoke to her about books, music, theatre, their friends…but he didn't allow things to be personal anymore. And he hadn't included her, thus far, in whatever he was planning.

Truth be told, she was nervous about that. Rhys was nothing but kind, but she'd learned the extremely hard way that a man could put on one face and live an entirely different existence. It was possible, however remotely, that he was planning something she wouldn't like. That he would take away her home and the child sitting before her.

She shivered, but was dragged from her thoughts when Kenley let out a shriek that could have broken glass and tossed the block down on the floor.

With an arch of her brow, Phillipa got on her hands and knees and playfully moved toward him. "Are you in the very worst mood?" she asked. "Perhaps because it's your…naptime?"

She said the last with great excitement, and that elicited a small smile from the boy before he shrieked again. She shook her head. Though she loved seeing him develop and grow, the increased lung capacity was…something.

"Mrs. Montgomery?"

She lifted her head to find Mr. Barton at the door. "Yes?"

"A letter has arrived."

He moved to where she still sat on the floor and she took it from him with a smile. But it fell when she saw the handwriting. "From my father."

Mr. Barton inclined his head, but she saw the tension in his face. Her father had visited this home a few times, and it had never been pleasant. She was embarrassed her servants…her friends…had to experience that.

"Shall I fetch Mrs. Barton to come get this boy?" Mr. Barton asked, and as he did so he made a funny face at Kenley. The baby clapped his hands together with another screeching squeal that made both adults turn their heads with a flinch.

"I think she's busy preparing that roast, yes?" Phillipa said. "I want her to focus on that—it's my favorite. I'll put him down."

"Very good, ma'am," Mr. Barton said before he waved one last time at Kenley and then stepped from the room. "Pardon me, my lord," she heard him say from outside her view in the hall.

She stiffened and glanced back toward the door as Rhys stepped into the parlor. His gaze flitted over her sitting on the floor, and she thought the corner of his mouth twitched like he was suppressing a smile. When he glanced at Kenley, the expression became more uncertain.

It was evident the man didn't have much experience with children. Not that it was an uncommon thing. Most members of the Upper Ten Thousand didn't have much relationship with their offspring at all, let alone other children. At her father's assembly she remembered a duke and a marquess once arguing over how many legitimate children they each had. They'd even placed a bet on it. Neither had guessed correctly.

But as she watched this man, one so unlike the others, she realized he was capable of much more. She swept up Kenley and got to her feet. He tapped on her face as she carried him toward his uncle.

"Good afternoon, my lord," she said and, without preamble, set Kenley in his arms.

For a moment they both froze. Rhys looked abjectly terrified and Kenley uncertain. But then the child lifted his pudgy hand to touch Rhys's chin, and Rhys...smiled.

Her breath caught watching them together, watching him relax as he began to rock Kenley, answering back to the baby's meaningless gibberish. She laughed at his enthusiastic, "Oh, yes? Tell me more."

"You're a natural," she said softly, and he glanced at her. His bright blue eyes caught hers, and in that moment she realized she was in love with this man. She was in love with the Earl of Leighton, her late husband's half-brother, a man she could never have.

And yet she loved him.

He tilted his head as he looked at her. "Are you well?"

She faked a smile. "Very well, thank you. I assume you didn't come into the parlor to have me force the sweetest boy in England on you." She squeezed Kenley's cheek and he turned his face into his uncle's shoulder with a shy giggle. "Did you need something?"

He cleared his throat and his gaze slid away from her. "Er, yes. I did come to talk to you about some things I've found. I have some thoughts for the future."

The area around her heart felt like someone was squeezing, but she ignored it and held out her arms for Kenley. "Let me put him down for his nap and then I'll join you." Kenley reached for Rhys as she took him. "Unless you'd like to...to join us? See his afternoon routine?"

Rhys hesitated, but then he nodded. "I would like that. Lead the way."

~

Rhys wasn't certain what had caused the shift in Phillipa, but he felt it all the way down to his bones. She had been looking at him in the parlor and then something had changed in her. A transformation in the way she stood, in the spark in her eyes. If only he could read that wonderful mind of hers.

But he couldn't. And he shouldn't. It wasn't his place, they'd very much established that.

Now she bent over Kenley as he lay on a little table in his nursery, changing him as she spoke softly, calming the baby with her voice and her touch. She lifted him from the table and held him to her shoulder as she began to walk to the room. She glanced at Rhys sometimes, but then away.

Kenley's eyelids drooped, he rested heavier in her arms. She laid him in the cradle, tucking his blankets around him, placing a stuffed rabbit toy against the crook of his arm. She leaned down and kissed him.

Before they left the room, she turned down the lamps and took one last glance at the child. Rhys felt her love for the boy in every single part of her. And he wondered at it, just as she had when she told the story of how she'd come to discover Kenley was her husband's bastard son.

That she could so deeply love someone that could only be a reminder of pain was a testament to her character, to her heart. She loved with depth and loyalty. He envied anyone who received that gift from her.

As they walked down the hallway together, he cleared his throat. "You are very good with him."

She shrugged. "It is easy to be. He has a happy spirit and is a very loving child." She laughed. "He does have his moments, though."

Rhys glanced at her from the corner of his eye. "I do not know much about children, I fear. But I believe what I just saw you do is often the duty of a nursemaid."

She slowed her steps and he saw that the question troubled her. "I...suppose in many houses, especially those with money and means, that is true. I've known of mothers of rank who sent their children off to wet nurses and didn't see them again until they were fully weaned at two or even older. But I would not wish such a thing." She followed him down the stairs before she added, "We live a small life here, Rhys. And I like caring for him."

"He is like your child," he said.

She bent her head, and for a moment he saw the streak of pain that had accompanied this very subject a few days before. "Only he is not."

He nodded. "One of the very topics I would like to discuss." He motioned to the study, which they had reached at last. "Please."

She entered the room before him and crossed to the chairs before the fire. As she sat, she declined tea or something stronger and just stared at him. She looked...petrified. Her hands gripped against the chair arms and her skin was suddenly pale.

"Phillipa," he said as he crossed to her. He sat in the chair beside hers and caught her hands. "What is it?"

"You are going to take him away, aren't you?" she gasped out.

His mouth dropped open and he stared at her in utter horror. "No," he said. Tears filled her eyes, and he continued swiftly. "I do not know what I have done to make you think of me so cruelly, but I would *never* take that child from you."

She bent her head, her breath coming in great heaves. "Oh, thank

God. You were so private about whatever you were doing and then you were talking about nurses for Kenley. I thought...well, you know what I thought."

"This is not a burden you should have to shoulder," he said softly. "And if you did not wish to be a part of that boy's life, it would be understandable. But I would never take him from you. Never. I can see how much you mean to each other."

"Of course," she said, and her fingers brushed against his as she took her hands away. "You have never proven yourself to be so cold. But with no information, I can run wild with potential futures, some of them not very good."

He winced. He had been trying to spare her these last few days, but instead had tortured her. "I am so very sorry, Phillipa. Let me ease your mind completely by showing you exactly what I have been doing these last few days. And by promising you that I will involve you in any other work I take care of that has to do with Kenley or with you."

As he stood to gather his papers, she stared up at him. "You—you do not owe me that."

"I owe you more," he declared, and then began to spread the paperwork out on the desk.

He motioned her to join him and she stood at his side, tantalizingly close. He could scent her skin, soft floral like spring embodied. He cleared his throat as if that could make him stop thinking of her in terms of poetry.

She was looking around as he organized, and shook her head. "I was so worried when I came in, I didn't even notice how much you've tidied up in here."

He followed her gaze. "Yes, I filed as I went through the papers, moved the furniture to where it actually made sense. I hope you don't mind."

She was silent a moment. "The room looks more like you than him now."

That sentence stung and he caught his breath against it. "I can put it back," he began.

"No." She held up a hand. "I much prefer this."

He didn't know what that meant. If there was something deeper to that preference. But there was no way to ask her. To demand she tell him that she wanted him when they had already declared they could not even kiss.

So he focused on what was before him instead of the desires that pulsed in his heart. "I, er...I suppose we must begin any discussion about Kenley's future by addressing the subject of Rosie Stanton."

"Yes," she said softly. "After she murdered Erasmus, she fled. Has there been any news on where she's gone?"

He heard the tension in her voice with the question and didn't blame her. "My sources in London have reported to me that she might have been seen boarding a ship bound for the continent. But it was a vague testimony at best. In truth, I do not know her whereabouts or her plans."

Phillipa clenched a fist against the papers on the desk. "I admit that makes me very nervous. Kenley is Rosie's son. And she loved him. I saw that in the way she interacted with the boy. But..."

"But she also murdered Erasmus in a fit of rage," Rhys supplied for her. "Not that I entirely blame her for that. But she was neck-deep in his schemes when it came to his bigamy and financial dealings. And she intended to help frame Abigail for crimes she didn't commit. Should she be able to raise her child with such a history? Would she be a good influence?"

"I don't know," Phillipa whispered. "I admit I wake up some nights, sweating at the idea."

The concept of Phillipa sweating in her bed distracted Rhys for a fraction of a moment, but he managed to rein in that reaction and concentrate on the very important matters at hand.

"It may be that we will never have to consider that future," he said. "Rosie Stanton ran away and she might never come back. I will continue my investigation. Owen is working hard on our behalf to do just that. But I believe we should carry on planning for a future that does not involve the woman."

"And what does that look like?" Phillipa asked.

He sighed and pointed to the ledger on the desk. "A great deal of my time has been spent on the financials. My brother was never very good at figures and when one is trying to grift for all one can, it doesn't make for sound financial planning."

She glanced down row after row of red figures. Debts owed all over the country. Loans taken to pay one collector, multiplying each bad decision.

"Great God," she whispered. "No wonder he locked the room up so I couldn't find this. So I couldn't see. Are those references to all the wives in the margins?"

"Yes, he was marking off dowries received in the income section, if you will look here." He pressed his lips together in disgust. "With every revelation of his behavior, my stomach turns."

"It is dire, I can see." She glanced at him. "What are your thoughts?"

"Well, I must take care of all these debts," he said, and the weight of that pressed down on him. "Do not worry yourself."

She pivoted and faced him fully. "This is me you are talking to, Rhys. I might not have to worry, but I can see your concerns written on every line of your face. Unburden yourself. Tell me how bad this truly is."

He cleared his throat. When she stared up at him like that, her green gaze steady and true, he felt as though he could tell her anything. He *wanted* to tell her everything. She was a siren that way, calling him to her.

"The House of Leighton is not a poor one," he said slowly. "But we are not the richest, either. I will not lie and tell you that this will not…change things for me."

Her expression softened and she reached for him, tracing her fingertips across the top of his hand. "I am more sorry than I can express. You didn't deserve this, Rhys. None of us did."

"Deserved or not, it is mine to carry and I will carry it," he said, catching her hand and folding it between his own. Her fingers flexed against his palm and it sent a shot of awareness through him. And peace. When she touched him there was peace, even in this gathering storm.

"Is there anything I can do for you?" Her voice was soft because they were so close. He stared down into her beautiful face and saw a thousand ways she could comfort him. All of them went against the rules they had put up, the walls they had erected a few days before.

"I would like you to carry on with Kenley," he said. "Here in Bath. I will take care of the debts on the house and cover all the expenses."

She withdrew her hand from his. "Oh. I see."

Her tone was suddenly flat, and he wrinkled his brow as she paced away from him to stand at the fire.

"You don't want to stay in Bath?" he pressed. She didn't answer. "When I came into the parlor earlier, I overheard that you had received a letter from your father."

She jolted as if she'd forgotten and dug into her pelisse pocket for the note. "I was distracted. But yes."

"I know it is complicated with your family," Rhys urged gently.

"That is a polite way of saying it," she said. "Let me read what he has written."

He watched as she broke the wax seal and unfolded the papers. It was not a long letter, that was apparent from the scratched-out words he could see on the paper, even from a distance, but she stared at it a long time. When she finally shifted her gaze to him, there was no color left in her cheeks.

"He is…he's coming here today," she stammered. "Without warning, without invitation. He says he will be here at two and it is…"

Before she could finish, there was a light chiming from the clock on the mantel. Two dings. And, as if conjured by the devil himself, at the same time there was a loud, insistent rapping on the front door down the hall.

CHAPTER 9

Pippa couldn't feel her arms. That had always been one of the many physical manifestations of the anxiety her father caused her. When he was angry, when he was cruel, it was as if it sank beneath her skin and caused a reaction in her body.

She had no doubt he would be cruel today. Their last interaction, that letter she'd received in London, had been the worst one ever. She didn't want to repeat it in person. But what choice did she have?

His voice boomed in the foyer—he was shouting at Barton, demanding he see her.

"I will ascertain if Mrs. Montgomery is in residence, sir," Barton said, his voice muffled and far away.

"She's in bloody residence and I will not wait." Mr. Windridge's steps pounded as he walked, Pippa assumed, into the front parlor to wait.

Pippa bent her head, cheeks burning that her father would bring that cruelty down on her poor butler's head. She couldn't look at Rhys, not right now. Not ever again, perhaps.

But of course he didn't allow that. He moved toward her and his finger slid beneath her chin. He forced her to look at him, be centered by the soft blue of his gaze.

"I am coming with you," he said. "You won't be alone."

Her legs almost went out from beneath her at that statement. She had felt so alone all her life. Even with others, even with the other wives, her friends, she didn't feel completely part of a group. And yet this man offered her solace, solidarity, acceptance.

"He will be wretched," she whispered, and hated how her voice broke.

Rhys smiled down at her and his fingers stroked the line of her jaw. *"That* is why I'm coming with you."

There was a knock on the study door, and Rhys stepped away as Barton put his head into the room. The butler's jaw was set. "I deeply apologize, Lord Leighton, Mrs. Montgomery, but you have—"

Pippa stepped closer. "Yes, I heard him. I am so very sorry, Barton."

He inclined his head and set his shoulders back. "I can put him out on the street if you would prefer, ma'am."

She smiled at the loyalty. "I would never ask you to do such a thing. I will see him, but you and Mrs. Barton needn't trouble yourself with any pleasantries. I do not think he will want the hospitality my home has to offer."

"Then I will stand by at the door to show him out," Barton said, and gave her a sharp nod before he departed and left her alone with Rhys.

She made a weak half-smile. "As you can tell, my father has been a difficulty many times in this house. I offer you a chance to renege on your offer to stand at my side. I would not blame you for the avoidance of him."

Rhys ignored the offer and held out an arm. She stared at it for a moment and then slid her hand into the crook of his elbow. His arm was strong, she could feel the muscle flexing beneath his jacket as he guided her from the room and down the hall. With every step she felt like she was being taken closer to the gallows.

At the door to the parlor, Rhys stopped. He glanced up the

hallway behind her and then the opposite way. When he was certain no one could see them, he stepped a little closer, too close, and smoothed his thumb against her jawline again.

"I wish I could do something to ease this tension," he said softly.

She swallowed hard because her mind automatically created the scenario where they didn't go into the parlor at all, but to her bed. Which only created a tension of a different kind inside of her.

And like he read her mind, his jaw clenched a little. "You are impossible," he whispered, and then he dipped his head and kissed her. Right there in her hall with her father behind the door.

It wasn't like the other kisses, where passion had been just under the purpose, teasing her with what else could be. This one was gentle, meant to soothe, although it did enflame all the same. She gripped his forearms to steady herself and leaned into him, soaking in his strength and his support and the way he made her feel so alive with just one touch.

When she pulled away, the anxiety of seeing her father had faded a little. That was what this man she loved could do with just the briefest touch. She smiled at him, wobbly but sincere, and then drew a deep breath and opened the door.

Rhys hadn't meant to kiss Phillipa. That seemed to be becoming a personal refrain, because it kept happening. But God's teeth, having her in his arms was worth all the pain he knew would follow at some point. He pushed that aside, because the pain she was about to face was far more present.

He saw her settle herself before she opened the door. When she was nervous, she always gave her shoulders a little shake, as if she were willing strength into her body. And then she entered the room, with him at her heels.

The man he presumed was her father stood by the window, arms folded, facing the door as they entered. Rhys took him in with one sweeping glance before Mr. Windridge spoke. He was tall, though not as tall as Rhys, with fading blond hair much like his daughter's. His eyes were different, though, dark brown rather than her vibrant green. Still, Rhys could see the similarities from parent to child.

"How *dare* you come back here?" Windridge snapped as a greeting.

Phillipa flinched ever so slightly at the harshness of the question, but then she motioned Rhys forward. "Father, this is the Earl of Leighton. My lord, may I present Mr. Calvin Windridge, the owner of Windridge's Assembly."

Rhys stretched his hand out, though he had no desire to touch a man who caused Phillipa so much grief. He only did so to reduce that anguish as much as he could.

He could see Windridge's wheels turning. The man was trying to shift from anger to deference, and it was clearly a chore for him.

"Leighton, eh," Windridge grunted as he shook Rhys's hand briefly. "So you're the brother of the charlatan who took us all in."

Rhys arched a brow. "A fact I knew nothing about, I assure you, Mr. Windridge."

"Rh—" Phillipa began, and then stopped herself with a blush. "Lord Leighton found out about Erasmus's betrayal at the same time I did, Father."

Windridge snorted. "And just when was that?"

Her jaw tightened a fraction. "In London. I told you that in my letter when you demanded an explanation for the rumors coming to Bath. The one you never answered except to tell me that I was no longer welcome in your home."

Windridge shook his head. "What else was there to say?"

Rhys stepped between them slightly, angling himself as if he could protect Phillipa physically from the scars that were being created with words and cruel expressions. "Why don't we sit?" he suggested. "You've come to see your daughter, after all—there is no need to make it unpleasant."

Windridge snorted, but he flopped into a chair as Phillipa took a place on the settee across from him. Rhys hesitated only for a moment before he settled in next to her. He didn't touch her, of course, but he wanted to be near enough that she felt his support.

The action, though, sparked a reaction. Windridge arched a brow. "And just what is *your* relationship to my daughter, my lord?"

Phillipa stiffened at Rhys's side. "Father," she said softly.

Rhys locked his gaze with Windridge's. "I am the brother of the man who deceived her, sir. Despite that, I have the very good fortune of being her friend."

"Friend," Windridge breathed. "Is that what you call it?"

Rhys wanted so desperately to rise to the bait this horrible man was dangling before him, but he fought to control that desire. "If you are asking why I came to Bath with her, it is to resolve some of the issues still outstanding when it comes to the evil my brother did."

"The whelp, you mean," Windridge said with a roll of his eyes. "His bastard."

Rhys's jaw clenched and he exchanged a brief glance with Phillipa. Her brow was wrinkled, and she looked as confused as he did. "I beg your pardon?"

Windridge's look was dripping with incredulity. "Come now. You aren't going to pretend you don't know that child that lives in this house is your brother's."

"What do you know about it?" Phillipa asked. "He is my former maid's son."

Her father shrugged. "I saw them together once."

Phillipa's jaw dropped open. "What? When?"

"I don't know." Windridge waved his hand around, almost with annoyance. "Last year some time. When she was still swollen with the child. I had come to call and they were kissing behind the stable. Montgomery was touching her stomach, whispering in her ear. It was obvious."

Phillipa's breath came short and she stared at her father in what could only be described as pure horror. Tears had filled her eyes and she blinked furiously, as if willing them not to fall and make her even more vulnerable than she already was. "You—you knew that my husband was being untrue with my maid and you said *nothing* to me?"

"A man deserves his privacy in such matters," Windridge said. "Why should I interfere?"

"Because I'm your daughter and you are meant to protect me," Phillipa gasped out. Her breath came short and labored for a moment, and it took every ounce of willpower in Rhys's body not to take her hand.

He should not have been a witness to this display. It was private, after all, and he had not earned a place in Phillipa's life that should allow him this. But he was glad he was here. Glad he understood, better than ever now, what this woman had endured her entire life. How it might have led her to see Erasmus as an escape route.

It put that ill-fated marriage into a very different light now.

Phillipa had calmed herself now. Her face was entirely serene even if her eyes were still lost and filled with broken-hearted betrayal. He rushed to speak so she wouldn't have to. "Although I will not comment to you, sir, about the state of that child's parentage, I admit he is part of why I've come. But I would think your greater concern would be how I intend to set things as right as they can be for your daughter."

Windridge let out another of those cruel little snorts of derision and shook his head. "Set things right? You know, you look like a clever fellow, but I wonder if you are actually daft. There is no setting things right for Pippa. She made a bed with her choice of a partner and she will lie in it in the end."

"It wasn't entirely my choice, though, was it?" Phillipa said softly. "You wish to absolve yourself, to blame me entirely, but we both know what really happened."

She pushed to her feet and paced away to the fire. She stood there for a moment, still fighting that gallant fight to control her emotions. When she faced them again, she was almost serene.

"We can go around and around forever about whose fault my sad marriage was," she said, and her gaze flitted toward Rhys before it darted away. "But it doesn't matter anymore. It happened. My larger question is—why are you here? You made it more than clear in your last letter to me that you want nothing to do with my life. Do you only come here to witness my suffering?"

"Your suffering?" Windridge repeated with a slam of his palm against the arm of his chair. "Selfish girl. You think you are the only one to suffer?"

Phillipa tilted her chin up in that defiant display of strength that Rhys had been captivated by since the beginning. "Far from it," she said, soft but powerful.

"That's right. Your mistakes impact *my* business," Windridge snapped.

Rhys jerked his gaze back to the man in shock and horror. "You compare whatever you have gone through to what she has endured?"

"My business has dropped all summer, since the truth of Erasmus Montgomery came to light."

"And you blame *Phillipa* for that, despite the fact that she is a victim of my brother?" Rhys asked with a cock of his head at the foolish logic of that statement.

"*Phillipa* should have been more careful."

"That isn't what you said two years ago," Phillipa said as she folded her arms, Rhys thought as a way to protect herself. "You were after me to marry a man who would elevate you and your salon for years. How many men did you all but throw me into the path of at your precious salon? Erasmus looked like a golden prize to you as much as he looked true to me. You and Mother were supportive of the union."

"Don't bring your mother into this. She's hardly left her bed since word reached us."

Phillipa's mouth tightened. "Yes. I recall how she reacts in those moments when she is so *very* upset. I was not the only cause of them."

Her father jumped up at that and snatched her wrist. Rhys didn't think, he just acted. In a breath, he was also on his feet, peeling Windridge's fingers from Phillipa's wrist.

"Don't touch her," he said slowly and succinctly as he pushed Windridge away from her.

There was a moment when there was only silence as Phillipa stared at her father, Windridge stared at Rhys and Rhys held that stare with a hard, heavy one of his own. But then Windridge stepped away, his face lined with disgust.

"I can see there is far more here than I imagined," he sneered. "Be careful, daughter." He smoothed his jacket. "I came here to see you for myself," he explained. "And now I have."

"And I assume to tell me that you will not see me again," Phillipa said softly, so very softly, almost like the words hurt her and she didn't want to give them more power.

"I will *not* see you again," Windridge said. "Nor will your mother."

Rhys set his jaw even harder. "You cannot mean that, sir. You cannot break with your daughter because someone else did something so cruel." He said the words as a way to protect Phillipa, but he was beginning to realize that her life might be better on every level if she never saw this horrid little man again.

"I have a business and a reputation to uphold, my lord," Windridge said. "As do you, I think. It is best, in these situations, not to allow anything...or anyone...to poison our chances." He glared past Rhys at Phillipa. "If you insist on remaining in Bath, I must ask that you do not ever associate yourself with my name again. *That* is what I came to tell you. And now I will go. Goodbye."

He said nothing else, he waited for nothing else, he simply pivoted on his heel and exited the room. Phillipa stared after him, green eyes wide, her entire expression dull and almost numb.

Rhys moved to the door, shut it so she couldn't hear her father screeching at Barton in the hallway. She flinched slightly at the quiet click of it closing and turned her back toward him. Her shoulders slumped and she gripped the mantel with both hands, her fingers curling against the edge.

And though it was no more his place than it had been a few moments before, now he couldn't stop himself from crossing to her. He placed his hands on hers against the mantel and she leaned back against his chest as her breath came shorter and faster.

"Phillipa," he murmured, close to her ear. She pivoted into his chest and he folded his arms around her, holding her as she cried softly and briefly. As if she didn't think she deserved to completely lose control, or feared the emotions washing over her at last.

"I'm sorry," she whispered. She tried to back away, but he held her firm as he tucked a finger beneath her chin and made her look at him.

"You never have to say you're sorry to me," he said.

Her gaze was soft and held his for what felt like an eternity. Then it slid lower, focusing on his mouth. She licked her full lips, and he was lost. All his reasons for distancing himself fell away and he bent her head and claimed her mouth, promising himself this would be the last time. Lying to himself because he knew it wouldn't be.

She lifted into him, a soft groan escaping her throat as she opened to him and their tongues merged with increasing passion. This kiss felt different. This kiss swept away reason and honor and duty.

This kiss felt like a prelude to all the delicious things he wanted to do to this woman. A prologue to a loss of control that would change everything between them.

He had to stop it. The reasonable, rational part of him roared at him to do so and with great difficulty he tried to pull away. She held tight this time, keeping their mouths a hairsbreadth away.

"Please don't refuse me," she murmured, her breath stirring his lips in the most distracting way. "Please don't."

"Phillipa," he groaned. "It isn't about what I want. It's about what's right...what's fair..."

"You already told me nothing about this is fair," she said, and let her lips nudge his jawline. "We are both suffering and we will continue to suffer. Why can't we comfort each other? We both know it can't be more than that. But why can't we just have...*this?*"

She was a siren, drawing him toward the rocks. He knew it, but wrecking himself was going to be magnificent. He needed it, needed her, more than he needed the propriety that he struggled to maintain. So he pushed aside the voice he'd followed his whole life, the one that said honor and prudence and pride.

"We're going to my room," he said, catching her hand and drawing her from the parlor. "I'm not doing this anyplace where we could be found."

She flinched as she stumbled up the stairs behind him. "Don't want to risk your reputation."

"No," he said with a glance behind him. "It's just that there are things I want to do to you, Phillipa. And what I want to do to you shouldn't be interrupted."

CHAPTER 10

Phillipa was shaking as Rhys drew her into his chamber. Shaking with need, shaking with anticipation, and yes, shaking with fear. Rhys seemed to note it even as he shut the door behind them, pressed her against it as he turned the key.

"Do you want this?" he asked.

She didn't answer with words. She couldn't find any. She just reached for him, drawing him to her, claiming his mouth with all the passion she'd tried to restrain for weeks.

Right or wrong, she wanted to explore it now. Perhaps for the only time, considering what was happening in both their lives. This was a stolen moment and she intended to revel in it.

He turned her, backing her toward the bed. As they staggered across the room, his fingers fumbled with the buttons along the back of her gown. He worked them free and stepped away from her as he tugged the dress forward, pushed it down around her waist.

And stared at her.

She blinked under the focus of his regard. The dark need that sparkled in his stare was so powerful, so tempting. She never wanted it to go away. She wanted this man to look at her this way for the rest of her life. He couldn't. He wouldn't. So she savored it now by sliding the gown the rest of the way down and standing before him in her underthings.

"Phillipa," he murmured, and his eyes roamed over her slowly from head to toe.

She fought not to shift under that focused regard, but it was nearly impossible. She'd never been particularly comfortable in her own skin. She'd enjoyed sex with Erasmus, at least at first, but her nudity had always made her blush.

She felt that same heat creeping into her skin without even removing the rest of her clothes, and found herself lifting a hand to cover herself.

He shook his head as he reached for her, dragging his fingertips down her bare arm. "You don't need to hide from me," he whispered. "Never hide from me."

She nodded and forced her hand away. He caught her waist and pulled her against his chest again, his mouth finding hers with hungry desperation. She unbuttoned his jacket and shoved her hands into the warmth of him, letting her palms explore against his linen shirt, finding strength in the body she had been fantasizing about for weeks.

He grunted, a sound of masculine desire and approval, and pushed the jacket away. He unwound his cravat awkwardly, trying to keep kissing her as he did so, and she found herself laughing at the attempt. He smiled against her lips and managed to drop the length of fabric aside. His hands slid into her hair as it fell and he angled her mouth against his more firmly.

She loved the flavor of him, mint and tea and desire. She wanted to memorize every note of it, like he was a fine wine uncorked at last for her to enjoy. It would be fleeting, but she wanted to get drunk on him nonetheless.

He seemed to want the same, and for a short time it was just tongues tangling and teeth clicking, seeking fingers unfastening and unhooking. At last, she pushed away, panting with desire, and watched as he tugged his shirt over his head. She caught her breath.

He was delicious. She'd felt the implied power of him when she held his arm or when he embraced her, but there it was, proven by the sculpted curves of muscle and sinew. He had a lean strength to his body, with muscled arms and a flat stomach. Chest hair lightly peppered his pectorals and a thin trail trickled down his stomach and into the low waistband of his trousers.

She reached out, hand shaking as she traced that line with one finger.

"What are you thinking with that look on your face?" he murmured.

She glanced up to find him watching her intently. She smiled weakly. "I'm wondering if you are real or some long dream I've conjured up to get me through this impossible time. I'm wondering if I'm going to wake up before I get everything I want."

He caught her waist and brought her closer. "I'm very, very real, Phillipa. And I'm going to give you everything you want."

He leaned in to kiss her, but she dodged his mouth. Instead she held his gaze as she grasped the waist of his trousers. She let her hand slide down the front, feeling the hardness of him beneath the fabric. The tendons in his neck flexed as he clenched his jaw with a harsh intake of breath.

She watched him as she unfastened first one button on the placard front, then the other, and let the fabric fall away. She slowly let her gaze come down, and her body clenched.

It was a very nice cock. Not that she had many to compare it to, and not that she wanted to make *that* particular comparison in this moment, but there it was. He was hard, fully hard and the long length of him curled up toward his stomach. She caught him in hand, stroking once, twice, and reveling in how this man who kept himself always in control dropped his head back and made a sound that was almost inhuman.

She stroked her thumb across the head of him, sliding a drop of his essence across the soft flesh. He surged into her hand, and in that moment the control snapped. Animal heat, more dangerous and powerful than anything she'd ever seen, took over the lines of his face, and when he cupped her cheeks and kissed her, she knew she was going to have pleasure beyond what she'd known before.

She surrendered to it, to him, as he stripped her chemise down her body with a hard tug. He lifted her against him, pulling one leg up against his hip as he placed her on the edge of the bed. His cock nudged her there, and she gasped against his mouth, ready for this and for him.

He seemed to have other ideas, though, because he didn't claim. Instead, he pushed her flat on her back. He looked at her, spread across his bed, her legs open, naked but for stockings and the slippers she hadn't yet removed. She had no doubt she looked wanton and wicked and ready to be used.

But she didn't feel ashamed. She *was* all of those things for this man, wanton, wicked, ready to be used by him, and *that* was exactly what she wanted to be.

"You are so perfect," he muttered as he caged her in with his hands, his gaze holding his. "Do you still want this? Want me?"

She nodded with so much eagerness that he couldn't have missed it. "Desperately, Rhys."

"Mmmm," he muttered with a smile. *"Desperately."*

He leaned in as if to kiss her, but instead his mouth found the side of her throat. He sucked and licked there, then lower, teasing and tasting across her collarbone and down her chest until he reached her breasts. He glanced up at her, watching as he cupped both of them.

She gasped at the feel of his warm hands on her so intimately. Gasped louder when he began to stroke his thumbs across her nipples, gently...then harder. Sensation started there and moved through her bloodstream, pumping between her legs, making her writhe against him.

He could have taken her. They were almost perfectly aligned, but he still didn't. He kept his attention on her breasts, continuing to pluck one nipple with his fingers as he took the other into his mouth. He sucked, hard enough to find the edge of pain, but not so hard as to send her over it. She mewled in pleasure, clasping her hands behind his head and holding him there so he could suckle and pleasure her further.

He didn't disappoint. He laved her and teased her and nipped her until she felt like a pool of molten lava, and then he did it all over again on the opposite breast. And just when she was panting and thrashing almost out of control, he slid his mouth away. Not higher to kiss her.

Lower. He moved his mouth lower across her stomach, lower along the curve of her hip. Lower to her thigh. He rubbed his cheek there, just next to her sex, and she gripped the coverlet in anticipation of what he would do next.

"So pretty," he mused, stroking a thumb across the lewd wetness between her thighs. She parted them farther, exposing herself more. He chuckled as he stroked her again, parting the outer lips, the tip of his thumb breaching her just a fraction.

"Please," she panted. "Please."

He nodded and peeled her open. He massaged those outer lips and sensation arced and zinged through her. Her cry was garbled and husky in the quiet of the room, then sharper as he settled his mouth there and licked her in one languid swipe.

No man had any right to be so good at this, but Rhys was. He dove into pleasuring her, licking and sucking like he'd done with her nipple. Only this time it was her sex, her clitoris, that he worshipped. He teased, but only for a short time. It was evident his drive was to make her come, and she felt so sensitive that it wasn't going to take much to get there.

He strummed her clitoris with his thumb as he licked her entrance, pushing back the hood and exposing the ultra-sensitive nub. She ground against him, shameless in need, begging him in with moans and gasps. He began to suck her clitoris, over and over in a steady pace. He murmured as he did so, the vibration adding to the madness as the dam of pleasure built between her legs. She flexed in time with him, her fingers digging into his shoulders.

The first wave hit her so hard that her vision blurred and she had to slap a hand over her mouth so her screams wouldn't be heard throughout the quiet house. She'd never come with such power in her life, and it went on forever because he just kept sucking her clitoris with relentless focus.

She was limp by the time it was over and he lifted his head from between her thighs. He surged up, catching her mouth again, letting her taste the earthy, heady flavor of her release. She grasped his hips as he did so, pulling him taut against her, demanding, yet again, what she really wanted.

And yet again, he didn't disappoint her. He reached between them, stroking the head of his cock against her wet entrance, aligning their bodies, and then he thrust, and he was inside of her.

It took a few gentle pulses to fully seat himself. She had been alone for a very long time and her body had to stretch to accommodate him. But when she did, it was electric. They were one body now, legs and arms tangled as he leaned her against the edge of the mattress and began to thrust harder and harder into her.

She clung to him, riding the waves of his loss of control, watching him as he came fully and completely undone inside and around her. He was no longer that proper earl, crushed by the weight of his responsibilities, trying to do what was best for everyone around him.

No, this was a different man. A man with hair wild from her fingers, a man with a hooded gaze thick with desire, a man with shining lips from eating her until she screamed...a man whose fingers dug into her flesh, bruising and claiming as he dropped his head into her shoulder with a guttural moan.

He yanked from her and ropes of thick release splashed across her skin as he pumped himself empty. He collapsed forward and she fell back. They were half on the high bed, half off, and she reveled in the heavy weight of him pressed against her.

For a moment, it was heaven and everything else fell away. But then he lifted his head and she saw the moment he shifted from Rhys her lover to the Earl of Leighton once more. His eyes went wide with...horror, that was the only way to describe it, and he stepped back from her, running a hand through already mussed hair.

"I am not my brother," he murmured softly, then repeated it, even more loudly. "I am not my brother."

She sat up. "Of course you aren't. I did not make that mistake, I assure you."

"*I* made the mistake," he said as he grabbed for his trousers. He yanked them on, fastening himself before he began to pace back and forth across the narrow room. He would not look at her.

"This was a mistake to you," she whispered.

That stopped him in his tracks, and he pivoted. "Not you. *You* aren't a mistake. I wanted you—God, I wanted you from the moment I met you and that little curl bobbed out around your cheek..." He trailed off and shook his head. "But I don't do this. A man can want things he shouldn't have and still have the honor not to pursue them. I do not take advantage like he did all his life. That is not me. It...it wasn't me until today."

She hesitated a beat before she slid off the bed. She was still naked, but somehow the embarrassment was fading. He watched her, pupils dilating as she crossed to him. She touched his face, and though he stiffened, he didn't pull away. He just stared down at her, the war he was waging deep within himself perfectly clear in those bright blue eyes.

She traced his jawline, then his lips with her fingertips before she lifted up on her tiptoes and drew his lips to hers. She brushed gently, back and forth, just a feather-light caress, not meant to spark desire, though it certainly did inside of her.

When she pulled away, she cupped his cheeks and poured all the love she couldn't say, would never be able to say, into him, hoping it would soothe him even if he didn't fathom what it was. "You didn't take advantage of *anything*, Rhys. You asked me more than once if this is what I wanted, and if I'd said no you would have walked away from me without consequences to me or my future. I wanted this as much as you did." She cleared her throat. "For as long as you have, though that admission may send us both to hell in the end."

His eyes widened. "From the first moment."

She smiled sadly. "Oh, yes."

There was silence between them then as they stood there, eyes locked, and a world of what could have been hanging between them. Finally he leaned forward and rested his forehead against hers. He shut his eyes and let out the longest, deepest sigh she'd ever heard.

"I wish things could be different," he murmured. "I wish...I wish so many things. But you know this is impossible."

She flinched, though it was only the truth he spoke. A truth she knew and accepted, despite the deeper feelings that tormented her heart. That was why loving him hurt so much. "Of course it is," she admitted. "I never believed anything different, Rhys. There are so many reasons why this can't work."

"My duty is to repair the damage Erasmus did," he said, she thought more to remind himself than her. "To you, to the others, to Kenley. To my own house and line, because at some point—" He moaned softly, as if what he had to say pained him. "At some point it will have to carry on and I do not wish to put a burden on my children."

"I know," she assured him. "The scandal surrounding what your brother did is enormous, and I am a part of that. I *know* what that means, I know that you couldn't throw away the consequences of this...this connection between us. I never expected you to."

There was relief on his face at that absolution, but it was immediately followed with regret. "Because, because, because...we could list a dozen reasons why we can't do this. Why we shouldn't have let it happen. Why it can't ever be more. I hate it, Phillipa." He reached out and cupped her cheek gently. "I hate every part of this and that it spoiled what was the most intoxicating experience of my life."

She smiled a little at that part of his admission. "The most intox-icating?"

He smiled back and that flutter of an expression made him look so much younger, so much more like the man who had risen up over her and taken her until they were both sweaty and shaking.

"Oh, yes," he promised. "I have never lost control like that with any other woman." His thumb smoothed across her skin. "God, it felt good."

"It felt amazing," she said. "I will never forget it." She shifted slightly. "You and I are not going to have many opportunities for something good just for ourselves in the future," she said softly. "You will have your duties to fulfill, and I will likely always be tainted by my past. Couldn't we just have…have this for a little while, Rhys? Don't we both deserve this something good after all we've been through and all we'll sacrifice before this is over?"

His cheek twitched. "You absolutely deserve more than one something good. I'm not sure I do."

She shook her head as she stared up at this man she loved and could not have. Not for more than a fleeting time. "Of course you do," she said. "I will tangle with anyone who says otherwise."

He chuckled. "Including me."

"Especially you, if you allow it." She laughed, too. "I thought that was what we were discussing."

His smile remained, though his laughter faded. "Oh Phillipa, you are a temptation. And I know myself well enough that one taste of you won't satisfy me for long. I will wake up tomorrow—hell, I'll go into a room tonight, and you will be all I see and all I need. If you are offering me a chance to surrender to that for a little while, I don't think I have the strength to deny you."

"Then I'm offering you just that." She leaned in closer. "Please, please, pl—" She didn't get to finish because he caught her mouth with his in a searing kiss.

His hands roamed down her back, cupping her backside as he lifted her up into him. He ground against her and she felt the hardness of him increasing, even through the thick fabric of his trousers. She shivered at that thought that this could be hers, he could be hers, just for a while.

He drew back at last, his breath short as he stared down into her face. "I think I better stop now," he groaned. "As much as that pains me."

"Yes. But I hope you'll leave your door open for me tonight?" she asked, shameless, and she didn't care.

He nodded. "Tonight and any other night you want to slip through it."

"Good. Now will you help me dress?" she asked, trying to keep her expression and tone light. "You made a bit of a mess of me."

He smiled as she began gathering up her things. Relief filled her...and regret. She'd get some of what she wanted, but not all. And she'd have to find a way to live with that.

CHAPTER 11

A few days had passed since the first time Rhys took her to his bed. Pippa had certainly been there every night since, where they learned each other's bodies and celebrated every kind of pleasure that could be given or received. In that bed, he was warm and wild and carefree.

Outside of it...well, that was a different story. He locked himself in Erasmus's office, going through the mess of papers. When he went into town, she was not invited, though she'd heard through Barton that Rhys had paid off most of his brother's debts and settled with other injured parties. He was methodically taking care of every loose end. When he was finished, he would be gone. And she had no idea what that meant for her, for Kenley, for the future.

She turned away from the window as Mrs. Barton entered the parlor, Kenley in her arms. The boy lit up as he saw Pippa, a joy she mirrored as she opened her arms to take him.

Mrs. Barton smiled. "He appears to have had no ill effects after the separation. You are still his favorite, it seems."

"Hmmm," Pippa said as she made a silly face at the baby and he laughed. "I am glad of it. Though I do wonder what he thinks of all this foolishness that has been his early life. He has lost so much between his father and mother, and now his uncle's entry into his life."

"Oh, but he seems very happy with that turn of events," Mrs. Barton reassured her. "Lord Leighton is not what I pictured, I'll tell you that. He's so warm with the child and with Mr. Barton and me. He's a true gentleman."

Pippa bent her head. Mrs. Barton was too observant of a person not to proceed with caution. "He is that."

Mrs. Barton shifted and glanced toward the door. "I do wonder, though..."

Lifting her head, Pippa saw that Mrs. Barton's face was lined with worry. Her throat closed. Here she had been focused so much on her own future, she had not put as much thought into what her servants must feel. They were in limbo as much as anyone else.

"You two are worried about the future," Pippa said, and reached out and took Mrs. Barton's hand.

"I suppose we must be, since none of us have any idea what Lord Leighton will decide."

Pippa squeezed her hand gently. "I will do *everything* in my power to influence Lord Leighton." She blushed at how that sounded. At how close to the truth it was. "I, er, I mean to say, that I will encourage him to ensure your future alongside Kenley's and my own. And it may be—it likely *will* be—that nothing will change for any of us. Lord Leighton will keep us here in Bath and we will go on as ever before."

Mrs. Barton nodded. "I suppose a man like that, kind as he is, wouldn't want to bring a scandal to London or his house."

Pippa froze. That would be, of course, the result of keeping Kenley in Bath. He would be hidden and his connection to the House of Leighton buried. But...Rhys couldn't want that, could he? He had, as Mrs. Barton said, begun to grow closer to the boy. He wouldn't shun him...would he?

As if conjured by those thoughts, Rhys, himself, entered the room. His gaze found Pippa first, burning into her with an expression she'd come to know well. It faded swiftly as he smiled at Kenley and then Mrs. Barton. "I have found the party at last," he said. "Good afternoon, ladies, Kenley."

Kenley began to gurgle and babble as he reached his chubby arms toward Rhys. And this man who had once hesitated when he saw his nephew now opened his arms as he crossed the room to take him. Kenley surrendered to him more than willingly, touching his face as he continued to babble in baby talk.

"My lord," Mrs. Barton said. "Oh, you're so good with that boy. I swear, I've never seen a man take so much to a child. So many are distant."

Rhys smiled, but Pippa could see the tightness to it. Something about what she said troubled him and that made her nervous.

"Well, I've preparations for supper to make," Mrs. Barton said. "Please ring if you need anything, my lord, Mrs. Montgomery."

They both nodded to her as she left. Once they were alone, Pippa leaned up. She kissed Rhys's cheek first and then Kenley's before she paced away to the fire.

"As much as I always enjoy a kiss from you, I'm sensing a bit of trouble. Do you want to discuss it?" Rhys asked as he set Kenley down on the soft carpet and handed him his favorite bird toy. The child immediately began crashing it up and down, making some approximation of a bird call. Though he hadn't yet formulated real words, he certainly liked to make sounds. Sometimes they all but echoed through the small house.

Pippa drew a deep breath as she faced Rhys. "I think I've been remiss in my duties and I was reminded of it today."

"Remiss in your duties," Rhys said, arching a brow. "That sounds very dire. Where have you gone wrong, Phillipa, and how can I help...or punish?" He winked, and everything in her warmed.

Except she couldn't allow for playfulness, not when it came to this most important topic of the day. She glanced at Kenley and gathered herself.

"We must talk about the boy, of course," she said. "You learn more about him and his life and habits each day. But I don't ask you about his...his future very often. I tell myself it is out of respect for your process in coming here, that you will reveal your thoughts when it is time. But I think, in truth, it is out of fear...and selfishness."

His expression grew serious. "Fear and selfishness are not ways I would describe you to anyone."

She ducked her head. "When I'm alone with you, I let myself be distracted. I *like* being distracted. That is certainly selfishness. And the fear...well, if you do not describe me as fearful, then I suppose I am hiding it well. I *am* afraid, Rhys. When I cannot see the path of the future, it is incredibly uncomfortable."

"I'm sorry," he said, and motioned toward the chairs before the fire. They sat so they could watch Kenley as he scooted around on his behind, swooping his bird and smashing his blocks together. Rhys sighed. "I've never been very good at sharing my plans or thoughts. For most of my life, I wasn't around people who cared much about them, so I learned to keep my counsel and simply do what needed to be done."

"I care," she said, probably as close to a confession of love as she would ever be able to make.

His expression softened. "Of course you do. It's in your nature. Your sweet, wonderful, very nosy nature."

She laughed at his teasing and it was like someone lifted those weights on her shoulders just a fraction. It didn't last, but oh, it was heaven.

Until he frowned and continued, "I've tried not to put all the complexities of my thoughts, the confusion of my plans, on you since I got here. I didn't think that it might make things worse for you rather than better."

She wrinkled her brow. "You and I have talked about this before. We are the only two who fully understand this terrible situation we find ourselves in. I *want* to be a part of the plans and thoughts, difficult or easy as they may be. Not just because it allows me a voice in my future and his." She motioned toward Kenley. "But because I want to help you, Rhys."

"You already do."

"In your bed," she whispered.

"Yes. That's the only time I forget all this."

"And I'm glad you can. I do too." She sighed. "But I want to do more than help you forget. This path is thorny. Let me help you navigate it."

He nodded. "The solicitor I hired here in Bath has been most effective in uncovering all Erasmus's debts. I believe they're all fully discharged now."

She flinched. "I heard you had done that. I hope it wasn't too high a price."

He snorted out a pained laugh. "Oh, it was. But it's taken care of. There was no alternative to that." He shook his head. "The rest of my time has been taken up with plans for Kenley. I've been working out what he might need, both for raising him and for educating him. As well as some kind of fund for when he is a man, to get him started on whatever path he chooses to follow. I want him to have choices and never despair."

"You don't want him to become reckless, like his father was," Pippa said. "Because you still blame yourself for that."

Rhys winced. "You know me so well. Yes. When my brother's behavior became untenable, I cut him off. And the removal of his income led him to the ruination of everyone around him."

"Because that was when he pursued and illegally married me."

His head dropped. "Yes. And then Celeste. And then pursued my best friend's sister as his fourth quarry. What I did led to pain for so many others. I don't want Kenley to ever have to travel that same path because I didn't provide for him."

Pippa reached for him, caught his hand and threaded her fingers through his. "Your brother's behavior is not your fault. It never was. And Kenley's will not be either."

He pursed his lips. "It's my duty to put him on the right path."

"Of course," she said. "But once he is a man, it is his responsibility to walk it. You didn't create the monster Erasmus became. That was born from years of dissolute behavior that he simply hid better. You did the right thing in cutting him off. A greater man than him would have evaluated that fact and changed, tried to prove himself to you. Rather than become an even worse version of what you accused him of being."

"How is it you can make things so easy?" he asked.

She shrugged. "May I ask you for a few details of what you would like Kenley's future to look like?"

He nodded. "Of course. You have a stake in it, I value your opinion."

"You mentioned funds for his future. For raising and educating him. What details did you establish for the latter?"

"Well, the best tutors, obviously," he said. "That will not come at a low cost, as they'll have to travel to him and likely stay. Not that Bath is such a terrible place."

She wrinkled her brow. "Tutors," she repeated slowly. "You mean when he is very young, I suppose."

He stared at her. "Yes. He is of the right age to have a nursemaid, you know that. You've been acting the role, as has Mrs. Barton, but as he grows up a bit, that will be difficult. That would be the first thing."

Pippa pursed her lips. "I do not mind being caretaker, Rhys. I like it."

"I know you do. I don't want to take anything away from you, only make it easier. You have a unique bond with the boy, but wouldn't you like help now and then? Wouldn't you like not to make so many demands on Mrs. Barton?"

She glared at him slightly. "You do know how to sling those arrows, my lord. I know you are right that I haven't been entirely fair to Mrs. Barton by asking her to take on so much with Kenley. I suppose having another hand, someone dedicated solely to him, would not be the worst thing."

"Very good. When he's four or five, I assume we'll hire him a tutor. That person might change over time, but I will make sure one is provided until Kenley is ready to go into the world, himself."

She blinked in confusion. "You do not picture that he would go to Eton or another boarding school for this primary education? Or on to Cambridge or another institution when he was ready?"

Rhys stared at her a moment, a brief hesitation that yanked her mind back to the earlier exchange with Mrs. Barton. That Rhys wouldn't want the scandal associated with publicly attaching himself to his nephew.

"Places like Eton, especially, can be difficult for boys who do not come from the ruling class. Truths like his are bound to come out. They could cause issues."

She folded her arms. "For Kenley...or for you?"

His nostrils flared and he tilted his head to examine her a little more closely. Then he got to his feet and stalked to the door, where he rang the bell. When Mrs. Barton arrived, he spoke to her a moment and the housekeeper came into the room and took Kenley and his toys.

"It's time for his nap at any rate," she said, her voice bright. She didn't seem to sense the tension that now pulsed between Pippa and Rhys.

All the better for it, and Pippa fought to control her temper during the few moments Rhys couldn't respond to her jab. When Mrs. Barton had left them, he shut the door and leaned on it. "I thought there was no reason for the boy to watch us argue," he said softly.

"Is that what we're about to do? Argue?" Pippa asked, though she already knew the answer to the question.

He took a long step toward her. "You implied that I would keep that child from an education in order to protect myself. Yes, I think we're going to argue."

"Isn't that what you're suggesting?" she asked. "A bright boy of a certain class goes to Eton."

"Very true," Rhys said. "Even those without means are sometimes given scholarships and join the ranks of their 'betters'."

"Then why deny your nephew the same opportunity?"

"How were you educated, Phillipa?" he asked.

She clenched her hands before her, trying not to view the question as an attack. "I-I had tutors, both generally and in specific subjects like dancing and comportment. I was educated to land a husband above my station. I learned a great deal from reading and asking what my parents labeled impertinent questions."

"Girls are not often sent away to school," he said softly. "Let me tell you that places like Eton can be hellish. Everyone knows who is there on charity or has a complicated past. Some of them thrive, yes, because they're likeable. Others are…tormented by bullies. So when I contemplate keeping Kenley from education outside of his own home, that is why."

The way he pursed his lips, the way his cheek twitched, it all made Pippa wonder what *he* had endured at Eton. But this was about Kenley, not the man before her. She shifted with discomfort. "I…I suppose I hadn't thought about what he might endure with his parentage and the scandals surrounding him. Do you really think that would come out?"

"Yes," Rhys said simply. "I absolutely do. Society works that way, and you know it after so many years of observation. Knowledge is power. Someone will put the pieces together."

She sighed. "It is a valid argument and I apologize for implying you had self-preservation as a reason for denying him. But please understand that good intentions or not, you *would* be denying him."

"Phillipa." He ran a hand through his hair as he at last shoved off the door and stalked to the window. She could see his upset in the way he shifted his weight, the way he fisted his hands open then closed at his side.

And yet she couldn't stop or comfort him. She had to plow on. "I want to see Kenley thrive and I *know* you do too. You've shown me not only in words, but in actions that you care about his future."

"I do," he admitted, seemingly through clenched teeth.

"Then consider, Rhys, will isolating him do that? A boy like him will not belong either in lower society or high, unless he is allowed to mingle in one or the other before he comes out into the world. Hiding him away in the countryside, it won't protect him. It will shelter him, and I assure you that those are two very different things."

She could see the wheels of his mind turning, and he bent to pick up one of the blocks that Kenley had tossed at some point during his playtime. He held it in his palm, staring at it like it might have the answers.

At last he sighed. "You are, of course, correct. In my hurry to protect him, I suppose my plans would be more likely to harm him. Which means they must change. There is a solution, so let me suggest it and see what you think, because it will affect you as much as the boy."

"What is that?" she asked.

"Come to London." He held her stare evenly. "All of you come to London and live there."

CHAPTER 12

The only sound that escaped Phillipa's lips as she stared at Rhys was a squeak. Not a word, not a witty rejoinder, just a squeak.

He arched a brow in surprise. "I have shocked you into silence. *That* is something."

"You have," she admitted with what seemed like great difficulty. "I almost cannot fathom what you are saying."

"Should I say it again, then?" he pressed. "Phillipa, will you come to London with Kenley?"

"So you go from hiding him away to parading him in public?" she asked.

"Not parading, certainly. But if the connection between us is bound to come out, then why not establish it from the very start?" He looked at the block in his hand, thought of the tiny fingers that had held it. Thought of the way that sweet child stared at him, smiled at him. "I would like to be close to him," he said softly.

Then he looked at her. If she agreed to this, that would mean being closer to her too. And God help him, he wanted that, even if he could never say it. *Should* never say it. It was so unfair to them both.

So he said something else instead. "There will be far more opportunities for him in London."

"I—" she began, but then her mouth just opened and shut.

"You and the Bartons will be given accommodation. I can think of a few neighborhoods that you would like very much and would be appropriate for a child of his situation and connection."

"Leave Bath…" she said softly.

He tilted his head and held her stare evenly. "Are you happy here?" he asked. "If you are, I can arrange whatever you like. I could make things better for you and still provide opportunities for the child."

He moved closer, drawn to her as he was always drawn to her. He reached out and stroked his fingers across the top of her hand. She sucked in a breath in response. God, how he loved when it hitched like that. The proof he had moved her, even a little.

"In London, you could see your friends," he said. "I intend to gift the house Abigail lives in to her, so she will be there permanently. And I believe Celeste and Owen will be there for his business. You could get away from the bad memories that this place must hold for you."

She dipped her head in response, and he knew he'd hit a mark. He slid a finger beneath her chin and tilted it back toward him. "You could be away from a father who might show up at any moment just to be cruel."

Her cheek fluttered a fraction and he saw the pain in her eyes. He hated that his words had put it there, or at least reminded her of its existence. He only wanted to soothe her, not harm her.

She backed away, turned her face, almost as if looking at him was painful as she said, "I can admit there are a great many things I would enjoy being…closer to in London. Would it truly be better for Kenley?"

He shrugged. "It will be different. There will be a great many tutors at our disposal in the city. I can make sure he meets the children of other men of importance, so he will have established friendships long before he finds himself at Eton."

"So he won't be an outsider."

"Correct," Rhys said. "And I can take a more hands-on role in his upbringing, for whatever that is worth. He can learn about the legacy of his family…both the good and the bad."

She did look at him now, almost like she was reading him down to the bone, though she had no right to do so. He had no right to want it so desperately. It was all so very unfair, what he wanted versus what he could actually have.

And her being close to him in London would only multiply that unfairness. But this wasn't about him and what would be good for him. There was a higher purpose to the offer. He would have to learn to live with the consequences.

"I can see how this would be better for Kenley," she said. "So yes, I will go to London with him. And I will ascertain if the Bartons would like to join us there."

Though this was merely a business arrangement, its purpose to help his nephew, a thrill worked through Rhys that was much stronger than it should have been. He had to call on all the propriety he had practiced in his life to keep from shouting out in pleasure.

He cleared his throat and pivoted toward the door. "I shall begin making arrangements right away."

He would have left the room then, both to do just that and to collect himself, but Phillipa caught his arm. He felt the weight of each of her fingers through his jacket, down into the very marrow of him. She licked her lips and all was lost.

"Do you have to start right now?" she whispered.

He couldn't breathe as he stared at her, as a thousand thoughts zinged through him. Chief among them was that once they were in London, this would have to stop. So he had better enjoy it while it lasted.

He bent his head and caught her mouth in a kiss as answer, and drowned in the taste of her, the feel of her. It might not be the last time, he couldn't think of it being that...but he was still going to celebrate her like it was.

❧

So many thoughts were spinning in Pippa's mind, and when Rhys took her mouth, it did exactly as she wanted him to do. He emptied all the tangled reflections, all the edges of fear, and left only...him. Always him. She parted her lips, allowing him to delve deeper, and wrapped her arms around his neck.

He was warm and hard against her as he tugged her backward and they fell together on the settee. She ended up in his lap, and she shifted her skirts so she could straddle him. He cupped her backside as they kissed, massaging the muscle there, rocking her back and forth against him the way they both knew this would end.

But she wasn't ready for the end yet. Not the end of passion, certainly not the end of what they'd begun to build here in Bath. She couldn't think of that end, when he would become only her employer, when they'd see each other only to discuss matters with Kenley. When she would ultimately watch him marry someone else, perhaps even love someone else, and would have no choice but to be happy for him.

He pulled away and gazed up at her, his eyes filled with concern. "Please don't find someplace to go in your mind, Phillipa. Be here with me right now."

There was a desperation in those words. Something that told her he, too, was pondering all those awful futures. Somehow that comforted her, that she wasn't alone in anticipating the loss. It allowed her to push it away, to give to him and not worry about what would come next.

She cupped his cheeks as she kissed him harder, deeper. He made that sound in his throat, the one she loved, the one that said he would surrender. That all the decorum would fade and be replaced with something far more powerful. Far more base and animal. He would become a man only she saw. One she could pretend was hers for the all too brief time they spent in each other's arms.

No. That was what she was supposed to forget. She pushed at it, wishing it wasn't a constant drumbeat in her mind. He tugged her harder against him, and she realized they were both fighting the same war. Not against each other, but against the inevitable.

She pulled away this time and stared down at him. They were both panting, both gripping each other because they were both seeking a lifeline in the undertow of reality. She drew a few deep breaths before she whispered, "We have now."

His expression softened and he nodded. "I don't want to spoil now."

"Neither do I," she said, and ground down more firmly against him. She felt the hardness of his cock against her thigh. A few small shifts and he could be inside of her, giving her pleasure, taking his own.

But that didn't seem enough today when everything was charged between them. She wanted to do something more, something just for him. So she inched away, off his lap, off the settee onto her knees on the soft carpet. He tracked her like a hawk tracked its prey.

"Phillipa," he murmured.

She shook her head. "Just let me," she asked as she slid her hands up his thighs. God, they were hard with tightly corded muscle. She pushed them apart, sliding between them as she unfastened the placard of his trouser front.

As she lowered it, he sucked in a harsh breath, and she looked up at him as she took his hard cock in hand. Making him come undone was intoxicating. She got almost as much pleasure from that as she did when he touched her. Almost.

She stroked him once, twice, and he squirmed a little, still an earl trying to remain in control. But when she lowered her head and gently touched the tip of his cock with her tongue, all that fell away. He rested his palm on the back of her head, not digging his fingers in and mussing her, but applying just enough pressure that her legs twitched.

If there was a silent demand in his touch, she acquiesced to it. She took him into her mouth, slowly at first, but edging deeper as she swirled her tongue around his thick length.

"Phillipa," he repeated, this time with more desperation.

She lived for that sound. That edge he was ready to fall over. She began to thrust her mouth over him, stroking the length of him that she couldn't manage to fit into her mouth with her hand. She started slowly, but built higher and faster, driving him toward a moment when he would either spend for her or he would catch her up, snatch back control and she would win all the pleasure.

He let her for a while, lifting his hips to meet her pace, his fingers tightening on the edge of the settee, knuckles whitening. But just as his legs began to shake, just as she felt herself dance to the very end of the wire of his control, he caught her upper arms and tugged.

His cock fell from her mouth with a wet pop and she let out a tiny squeal as he dragged her back into his lap. His mouth found hers, hungrier than ever as he shoved at her skirts.

"Ride me," he demanded low in her ear. "I want to feel you come, I want to see it on your face."

She didn't have to be asked twice, and she shoved her skirts aside and all but ripped the slit in her drawers in her haste to open herself to him. He caught her hips and guided her as she aligned their bodies.

Inch by inch she took him inside, to where she was already slick and ready for him. They moaned together as he stretched her, filled her. She tightened her thighs around his, reveling in the wickedness that they were both almost fully clothed, that they were in a public parlor, that this was not in either of their responsible natures.

When he squeezed his grip on her hips and rolled her forward as he thrust, she forgot all rational thought. She lost herself in sensation and did as he had demanded: she rode him. She ground herself down on him, stimulating her clitoris, she lifted up to tease him, almost sliding all the way away from him. She did it slowly, she did it faster, and after just a few moments they were both gasping. She gripped him harder, inner muscles already fluttering as the pleasure mounted.

And when she came, he caught the back of her neck, pulling her mouth to his so he could swallow her moans of pleasure as she jerked and writhed in pure sensation. He was on the edge with her there. She could tell by the way he nipped her lip, by the way he surged beneath her, by the way he panted her name. The strain increased on his face and she rode him through it, needing what he could give. Wanting it more than she had ever wanted anything or anyone.

But when his crisis arrived, he retained some control after all. He lifted her away, catching his cock beneath her skirts and covering it as he grunted out orgasm. She felt the faint splash of it on her thigh.

She watched him, fascinated, as he flopped his head back against the settee, eyes screwed shut, a peace on his features that she rarely saw. At least she gave him that gift. That rare escape from his troubles. It was all she wanted for him, it was something she mostly couldn't give. It wasn't truly her place to keep trying.

He opened one eye. "Are you trying to make a measure of me?"

She smiled as she slid from his lap and adjusted herself slightly. He tucked himself away, as well, and they were back to propriety, as if the passionate moments hadn't happened at all.

"I needn't make a measure, my lord," she said as she tilted her head and traced the line of his jaw absently. "I know who you are."

He held her gaze for a beat. For what felt like no more than a second. For what felt like a lifetime. And then he nodded. "Yes. I think you might."

She realized then that he loved her, too. She saw it in his blue eyes, she felt it in the way he rested a hand on her knee gently. It was in his body language, in the sound of his voice, in every part of him. He loved her. She loved him.

And none of it mattered. The past they shared would keep them from the future they couldn't. It took everything in her not to burst into tears right then and there.

Instead she forced a smile. "You were trying to escape me, I think, when I distracted you."

"In the most pleasant way, I assure you." With each passing moment, he regained some of his decorum. His tone returned to that of a proper earl, his posture changed as he got up and went to the mirror above the sideboard to ensure she had not mussed him too much.

He pivoted back and speared her with that blue gaze again. The one still burning with love for her, despite all other departures back to the man he felt he should be. "And I would never wish to escape you, Phillipa." He crossed back to her and leaned over the back of the settee to kiss her. She lifted into him, touching his cheek as the kiss deepened. When he pulled away, she was breathless all over again. He sighed. "I do have much to prepare for a departure to London, though. I hope we can continue this tonight?"

She nodded, smiling at him until he left the room. But when he was gone, the smile fell. The reality of what was about to happen was so loud and powerful that it felt like her world was quaking with it.

Going back to London with this man meant she would see him regularly. He would be a part of her life, she a part of his because of Kenley. But that would be all. There would reach a point, probably very swiftly, where they couldn't have long looks. They couldn't share stolen moments.

So she would love him from afar, and that would be all.

She bent her head, fiddling with a loose string on the settee cushion as she tried not to let that thought overwhelm her.

Tried not to be lost in how empty that future felt. For her. For him.

CHAPTER 13

Pippa had known that going to the shops wasn't going to be the most pleasant experience, but she had a few things she needed in preparation for the household's departure to London the next day. So here she stood, in the middle of her favorite bookshop on Milsom Street. This had been a haunt of hers all her life. She'd found a union with those who loved books as much as she did, and shared many a kind and lively conversation with those within these walls.

But today every other patron glowered at her from the corners of their eyes. They stepped away when she moved too near, as if she had a contagious disease. Scandal was certainly that, it seemed.

She sighed and gathered the books she had selected to take to the front of the shop. Mr. Wilson, the proprietor of the store, met with her there and his lips pursed. She was rather shocked to see it, as they had always had a cordial relationship before…well, just before.

"Mrs. Montgomery," he said, his tone icy cold.

"Mr. Wilson," she returned, trying to keep her voice bright, like she didn't notice that she was being shunned. "Would you put this on my account?"

He shook his head slightly. "I'm sorry, ma'am, but I'm afraid I can no longer extend you credit."

Her mouth dropped open and she gaped at him, wishing her cheeks weren't filling with heat as the entire shop turned toward her. "Mr. Wilson, I have always paid my debts on time, even early. You have never had to wait."

"Indeed," he said, and not softly. She knew the store at large was listening to this humiliation. "But your...situation has clearly changed. It would be better if you simply paid for what you would like."

Her jaw tightened and she carefully set the book in her hands down on the counter. "I have been a faithful customer here all my life, sir. And while I certainly have the funds to pay for my books directly, it seems I do not find hospitality here any longer. Good day."

She pivoted and left the shop in what she hoped was a dignified, yet indignant, cloud. But on the street, she blinked at tears. Here was her downfall, laid out in stark terms. The truth was, she could have paid for her books, but not if she also wanted to pick up a few items in the general store to entertain Kenley on the road. And since she had to assume she would find the same level of animus there, her credit retracted in the face of Erasmus's lies, she had to save her money.

She tried to calm herself as she walked up the busy street and entered the other shop. Once again eyes slid to her as she did so, and she thrust her shoulders back and ignored them.

She moved to the area where children's toys were stacked and picked through them. Mr. and Mrs. Barton had agreed to move with them to London, so the party would be traveling in two different carriages, along with a cart to carry their trunks and the few items of furniture that belonged to Pippa. Kenley would probably be passed back and forth between the travelers along the way. Still, it was a long journey and she hoped to find some new items to entertain the boy.

She picked through tops and balls, blocks and stuffed toys, choosing a few that she thought Kenley would like. She was about to take her items to the front when she realized that her mother was standing across the shop from her, staring at her.

Her heart lodged in her throat. If she had a difficult relationship with Calvin Windridge, the one she shared with her mother was even more complicated. Mary Windridge had always deferred to her husband's judgment on all things. She had never stood up for Pippa, nor offered much comfort when she had difficulty. It was something Pippa had come to accept, but as she stood there, staring at her mother, she knew she might never see her again.

And she couldn't help but move to her, flinching when her mother subtly flicked her head as if to ask Pippa to follow her. Then she turned away and hustled to the back of the shop, behind some shelves. It seemed Mary didn't want to be seen with her.

Pippa sighed and slipped into the more private area. Her mother stood in the shadows, wringing her hands together.

"Your hair looks very pretty," Mary burst out.

Pippa lifted her hand to her curls and nodded. "Thank you, Mama." They stood in awkward silence for a moment, and then Pippa let out a long sigh. "I am going to London. I think you must know that."

"Word has spread," her mother said softly. "You are the subject of a great many rumors, so yes, I have heard you are packing up your house here and departing."

"Father must be pleased," Pippa said. "He made his thoughts about me very clear when he visited last week."

There was a flash of regret across her mother's face before she shrugged. "He is a businessman, Pippa. And his business cannot abide rumor or innuendo. There are other assemblies, he is always competing. One wrong move from any of us—"

Pippa held up a hand. "Trust me, Mama, I recall every word of this lecture from my childhood, you needn't repeat it. I do understand that this situation puts him in a terrible position. I only wish both of you would understand that it puts me in a worse one."

Her mother stepped closer. "I...I do understand that, Pippa. Truly, I do. Your situation is untenable, and it is through no fault of your own. If I could help you..." She shook her head. "But I cannot, don't you see?"

"I do see," Pippa whispered. "No one can truly save me in the end. Going to London will be best for everyone. It will allow you two to distance yourself and, I hope, save whatever face is necessary to carry on here in Bath. And I will also start anew, in a place where I can eventually be much more anonymous."

Her mother worried her lip. "You won't be able to marry again."

Pippa stifled a humorless laugh. Mary had operated in a world where marriage was the only option. This social death of Pippa's had to weigh even more heavily in light of that.

"No, I think not," she said. "Even if a man were to..." She caught her breath and tried not to think of Rhys. "...to want me, there are a great many barriers. The scandal for one, my utter lack of funds for another. I shall go into service now, taking care of the child."

"Do not speak of such things so loudly," her mother hissed, and caught her arm.

Pippa gently shook her away. "I was not being loud, Mama."

Her mother sighed and bent her head. "How can that be tenable to you, to be responsible for a child who is the product of your late husband's imprudence?"

"Imprudence is putting it mildly," Pippa said. "But it is not that baby's fault, is it? No more than it is mine. His mother has vanished, his father is dead. It would be wrong to abandon him."

"As you have been abandoned by your parents, I suppose you mean?" her mother asked, her jaw tightening.

Pippa shook her head and refused to respond to that. If her mother felt some guilt over what was happening in their fractured family, Pippa had no desire to assuage it. At least not at the moment.

"I will be fine," she said instead.

"You might consider *all* your options, you know," Mary said, cheeks flaming. "The alternatives for making your way in London will be many."

Pippa wrinkled her brow. "What do you mean? I have no experience in any other kind of service and I have no references."

Her mother shook her head. "Not service, Pippa." She shifted and her gaze darted around as if she feared being overheard. When she spoke again, her voice barely carried. "Your father says *that earl*...your late husband's brother...he looks at you a certain way. You are a beautiful young woman, my dear. And men will take care of those who provide—"

Pippa staggered away a step as she realized her mother was suggesting she become a man's mistress. Rhys's mistress, specifically. "Mama," she gasped. "Thank you for the suggestion. I will certainly keep it in mind."

"He owes you," Mary grumbled.

"If you are still talking about *that earl*, as you put it, he owes me nothing," Pippa said. "He is far too decent to be maligned in such a way by you or by my father. I will do anything to assist him, as he has been damaged by this situation as much as any of us."

Her mother's gaze met hers and held there a moment. Pippa was horrified to see it filled with pity. "I see," Mary said softly.

"I think I should go now. I've much to prepare and I think you have already spent too much time with a pariah such as me. I will write to you from London."

Her mother shook her head. "It would not be wise, my dear."

Pippa stared at her for a moment as that statement sank in. Then she cleared her throat. "Then it appears this is goodbye. I wish you and Father all the best, Mama."

Her mother's eyes filled with tears. "And you, Phillipa. Goodbye."

Pippa turned and rushed to the counter, where she paid for her items, now oblivious to the eyes on her, to the whispers of her name as she left the shop, left her mother, truly left her life behind.

With no hope that the future would bring any more warmth or

hope than the past. And it took everything in her not to weep in the street at that thought.

CHAPTER 14

R hys glanced across the carriage toward Pippa and frowned. She had been very quiet since her return to the house yesterday afternoon. In fact, quiet wasn't the word for it. Except for polite responses to questions directly asked of her, or to make directives on what was to be moved or loaded that morning, she had been entirely silent.

And she had not come to his bed the night before. She had barely looked at him at all. Something had happened, *something* had changed, and he wanted to know what it was.

But he couldn't ask her right now. Mrs. Barton was riding in the carriage with them while Mr. Barton rode Rhys's horse outside the vehicle. And Nan had Kenley in the other, smaller carriage behind them, because he was napping.

But there was no privacy for what Rhys thought might turn into a very personal conversation. One he dreaded.

The carriage began to slow, and Mrs. Barton peeked out around the curtain with a smile. "Looks as though we've reached the inn. Lor' I can't wait to stretch my legs."

Phillipa flashed a brief smile. "Yes. It's a long ride."

Rhys cleared his throat. "But we did the bulk of it today. We're only a few hours from London now. We won't have to rush in the morning and will still reach the city before teatime."

"Excellent," Mrs. Barton said. "Mr. Barton and I are ready to take ourselves to the new accommodations and get everything ready for you."

Phillipa covered the housekeeper's hand. "You are too good to me. I'm so happy you're both staying on staff and willing to do that work."

Rhys also smiled at Mrs. Barton. It was a relief, after all. His solicitor in London had procured what was promised to be a nice home just on the edges of the West End, close enough to his home that he could reach them in an emergency, far enough away that he wouldn't be...

Tempted.

But the home was not fully ready, and so Mr. and Mrs. Barton had made the agreement to head there first and put everything right, while Phillipa and Kenley stayed with the original Mrs. Montgomery, Abigail. A fine arrangement all around, and yet he felt more and more anxiety the closer they got to the city and the ultimate end of the connection he and Phillipa had built.

The carriage stopped and that ceased his maudlin thoughts too, or at least slowed them. There was a bustle of activity as Rhys's driver clamored to arrange their accommodations and the Bartons and Nan joined together to get the items everyone needed for the night and Kenley inside. Which left Rhys to exit the carriage and turn back to offer Phillipa a hand out.

One she hesitated in taking. She also refused to meet his eyes as she set her feet on the ground and gently stretched her back. "This is a different inn than the one we stopped at on the way to Bath what feels like a lifetime ago," she said.

"That is the longest sentence you have said to me in twenty-four hours," he said softly.

Her gaze jerked to his face then and she blushed bright as a plum. "I...oh, I've been abominably rude, haven't I? I'm so sorry."

He shook his head. "You never need apologize to me, Phillipa."

She drew back slightly. "Of course I do. If I am wrong in my behavior, I must apologize to you first and most strenuously because I—" She cut herself off and her eyes dropped to the ground between them. "Because you are a friend to me."

He clenched his jaw. She hadn't been intending to say he was her friend. It was true, of course, that he wanted to be a friend to her. He liked that role very much. But it was bound so closely with the other part he'd taken in her life: lover. Combined together, they were a very dangerous thing. A good friend who was also an amazing partner in the bedroom…that was what every person secretly hoped for. That was, he feared, love. And he couldn't love Phillipa, not the way she deserved.

So he ignored the slip and motioned his arm toward the little copse of trees behind the inn. "There's a pretty path through the woods here. Perhaps we could take a turn together."

She worried her lip a moment, a most distracting action, and then she nodded. They walked together, not touching, toward the woods. "How did you know about the path?" she asked.

He shrugged. "I've stopped at this place before, returning to London from Leighton. It's past Bath, but it takes some of the same roads to get to the city."

"I always wondered about it. You never speak of it and Erasmus only said unpleasant things."

"I'm sure that's true," Rhys said with a frown. "After all, he very much resented that it wasn't his to inherit. He and his mother only had complaints about its dark halls and wild moorlands. It was too distant, it wasn't modern enough. There was no company that they appreciated."

"But you liked those things?" Phillipa asked.

He nodded. "I like London—I do spend most of my time there. And I do admit there is upkeep to the estate that will be…complicated by the current events."

She flinched. "The money you've had to put out to fix your brother's mistakes."

"Yes." He shook his head. "But when I wish to be alone, isolated, to just hear myself think...there is nowhere better in this world than Leighton. I wish you could see it, Phillipa. I think you'd love it. And as Kenley gets older, he can race along the same cliffs that I did. Probably get himself into trouble as I did and..."

He trailed off because she had pivoted to face him on the path and was simply staring at him. He realized what he was saying to her. That he was creating a picture of a future that could never be. Would never be.

"I'm sorry," he said softly. "I got carried away."

She shrugged and started up the path again. They'd reached the woods now and she sighed as she entered the trees. The sun was just starting to go down and golden light danced through the branches and cascaded around her like a halo.

"If you say I must never apologize to you, you certainly must not apologize to me. I like hearing about where you grew up. It sounds beautiful. I never had much experience beyond Bath and London. I suppose now I never shall."

He cleared his throat. "What upset you?"

She faced him at that abrupt change of subject. "Upset me?"

She was playing innocent, but he could see she knew what he meant. Why he had asked. Still, she was trying to erect a wall between them, one he probably should just leave alone, because he knew she did it as a kindness to them both.

Except he couldn't.

"When you returned from your outing yesterday, you were changed," he pressed. "You have hardly spoken since and I see something in your eyes. Something so very sad. Are you unhappy about going to London? Is there something I can do?"

"Of course you would wish to," she said with a shake of her head. "Because you are you. But you cannot, Rhys. There is nothing you can do."

"Would telling me help?" he asked.

She worried her lip again and God, that was distracting, even in this moment when he was so focused on her heart. Then she let out a very long breath. "I did not have a very good experience at the shops in Bath yesterday," she admitted. "And it made me realize, in a more complete way than I had allowed myself before, that this scandal has ruined me. Completely."

"People were rude to you?" he asked, and heard the tremble in his voice.

She nodded. "Very. Including people I've known almost all my life. People I've had a very reasonable relationship with. They practically hissed me out of the bookshop. And then later I saw...I saw..."

He moved toward her then, knowing he shouldn't, but he needed to touch her, to comfort her when tears filled her eyes. "Go on," he whispered.

"I saw my mother." Phillipa shrugged. "You haven't met her. She is not like my father, you know. She can be very dramatic when it comes to these sorts of things. Yesterday she wasn't. But she did make it very clear that any relationship we have had must be over. She does not even wish for me to write, I suppose because the association with me hurts their assembly hall."

"Wretched creatures," Rhys snapped.

She shook her head. "No. Well, yes. But the fact is that they are *right*."

"They are not right. You are their child, they ought to move heaven and earth to stand by you and defend you, especially since you are not in the wrong in the situation, but the injured party."

"And yet we are both well versed enough in the world to understand that fault rarely comes into play when scandal is discussed. I am linked to an infamous person and an even more notorious set of events." She shivered. "I carry fault in the public eye at the same level as the man I so foolishly married. I should never have hoped for more from my parents because of that. But..."

She trailed off and walked away from him, deeper into the woods where the only sounds were the faint chirpings of birds settling in for when night would fall shortly.

He stared at her there, her blue pelisse bright against the dark background, her curls peeking out from around her bonnet as she stared up at the trees like they had some kind of answer for her.

"You wanted them to be what you deserved." He felt every word like a stab to his own heart. "Not what they are."

She faced him. "Yes, I suppose I did, quite foolishly, want that. How did you know?"

"Because I felt the same way...so many times," he admitted.

She moved back toward him, her expression opening up a little. "How did you respond?"

"Badly," he choked out as she reached him. He couldn't resist touching her. He traced a gloved finger along her cheek and then wound a blonde curl around that same finger. "And eventually by turning to friends who knew my true value."

"Like the Duke of Gilmore," she said, but her breath was short now. She was as moved by being close to each other as he was.

He forced himself to think of his old friend rather than his ponderings of what he wanted to do to this woman in the quiet of the woods. "Yes," he said. "Somehow he is still my friend despite Erasmus's attempts to ruin his sister. He will offer nothing but support when I return to London, just as he always has."

She smiled, but there was sadness tingeing it. "I'm so glad you have a friend like that. You deserve him."

She moved to pull away, but he caught her hand and kept her there. "So do you, Phillipa. You deserve more than they've ever shown you or told you. You are worth so much more."

The tiny sound she made from the back of her throat, a combination of joy and grief, of pain and acceptance, he knew he would hear that ringing in his ears for the rest of his life. She eased closer and her hand rested on his chest as she stared up into his eyes.

"Rhys," she whispered.

He leaned down toward her, hungry to have her lips on his, to feel the physical connection that he feared would soon be gone. But before he could kiss her, there was a distant shout from behind them, then a burst of laughter from the men working. They both jumped, pushing apart.

"You forget how close the inn is," she panted. "When you're in the trees."

He nodded. "We...we ought to go back before we create even more scandal than already follows us."

"Yes," she said softly, he thought with a little defeat. "Come, I promise to be better company. It did help to say what happened out loud."

"Good," he said as he followed her back to the inn. And he was glad he had been able to assist her. But it all felt a little empty now. And he mourned all the things he wished to do but couldn't.

~

Pippa wasn't certain she had been better company the rest of the night, but she'd tried. She'd talked and laughed and shared her supper with the Bartons and Rhys. And all the while his bright eyes had speared her, turning her insides to mush just as they always did.

The fact that her love for this man was only growing was a tragedy, and yet it wasn't something she could change.

"I *wouldn't* change it," she corrected softly as she swept up the robe Nan had draped across the bottom of her bed just before she left her that night. The maid was sharing a room with Kenley so she could watch him. She had become so good with the boy that Pippa thought she might be better suited to be his nursemaid.

Pippa was just as happy to be alone. She was not good company between the dark feelings that still plagued her when it came to her departure from Bath. And the other feelings...the ones for Rhys... well, those made things difficult too.

He was just down the hall from her now. Three doors down, across the way. An easy distance to cross. If she went to him, he would accept her. She knew that. He wanted her, he loved her. Was it fair to trade on those things for comfort? Was it fair to break both their hearts over and over?

She was already moving to the door even if she didn't want to face those answers. Already going to him. But as she threw open the chamber door, she gasped. He was stood there, swathed in a silk robe, hand lifted as if to knock.

They stared at each other for a charged moment, and then he caught her cheeks, pulling her in for a kiss as he backed her into her room and kicked the door shut behind them. He locked it before he guided her to the bed.

"You were coming to me," he grunted between kisses as he fumbled with her robe tie.

She nodded against his mouth and slid her hand beneath his robe. He wore nothing under it and she hissed out a sound of surprised pleasure as her fingers tangled in the fine smattering of chest hair.

"I needed you," she admitted while he tugged her robe down, stripped her nightrail away and left her standing naked before him. He stepped back, staring at her, memorizing her, she thought. Just as she had memorized him so many times.

"I need you," he admitted. His voice was rough now, thick with desire and emotion and desperation she hated and craved all at once.

Their mouths met again, heated and driven. He slipped from his robe as he lifted her onto the bed, and then it was all skin on skin. She wrapped her arms around his shoulders, tugging him flat to her, shivering at the warmth of him. The strength. When he touched her, when he held her, he was the whole world, if only for a moment. She needed that, needed him.

So she let him. Let him be her center, let him be her heart, her soul, her everything. And pretended that it wouldn't end.

CHAPTER 15

Something in Phillipa shifted. Rhys couldn't identify exactly what it was, but he felt it in the way she relaxed against him. Like a war was over and she had surrendered. Their kiss softened, her fingers dragged into his hair. He cupped her hips and rocked her closer as she wrapped her legs around his bare hips.

He wanted to stay like this forever. This was freedom, these stolen moments with her. He didn't want to lose that or lose her. Because he loved her. That wasn't a shock to him. He'd known it for some time, even if he hadn't dared label it. But holding her now, feeling her breath quicken as he dragged his mouth down her throat, he couldn't deny the words anymore.

He loved her. He would always love her. It was just that, as had so often been true in his life, what he wanted didn't matter. That burned like a brand against his skin, but he ignored the searing pain. It was worth it to be with her again. But since it might be the last time, he needed to make it last. Needed to make it something neither of them would ever forget. Needed to make it something that could sustain him when everything became bleak again in London.

And so he tasted her, feasted on her skin as he somehow

managed to maneuver them both onto the bed together. He dragged his mouth to her throat, sucking on the spot where her shoulder and neck met. She flexed her fingers against his back as she let out a shuddering sigh of pleasure.

He dragged his lips lower, savoring the slight saltiness of her skin as he crested over her breast and rolled his tongue around her nipple. When she arched her back and let out a gasp of pleasure, his cock went fully hard. Watching her shatter was the ultimate aphrodisiac—he was addicted to it, to her, to what happened when they came together.

He swirled his tongue over and over, sucking and soothing as she writhed. As he did so, he let his hand travel lower, down the apex of her body, until he settled it between her trembling legs. She opened them, ready and wet and willing as he stroked his fingers across her heat. He pressed one inside, reveling in the flex of her tight body around him, in the way she made a garbled sound of wordless pleasure.

He fucked her with his finger, then two, pressing his thumb to her clitoris as he kept teasing her breasts, back and forth. Her hips lifted, her body clenched in time to his thrusts and he felt the slick heat of her increase as she ground toward release. He wanted it. He wanted to watch her as she found it. When she did, it didn't disappoint. Her back arched hard, her mouth fell open and she panted out a series of soft moans as her sheath rippled around his fingers. He drew out her orgasm as long as he could, and then he pulled his fingers free and licked them clean as he smiled down at her.

Her pupils dilated further and she shook her head. "I think you only pretend at being proper, my lord."

He smiled at the quip. "Then only you know my true self."

He'd meant it as a flippant reply, but the moment the words were out of his mouth, the air in the room shifted. She softened a fraction, and he bent his head. That was true, of course. He had shown so much more of himself to her than he'd ever allowed with any other person.

But he didn't want tonight to be about what they couldn't have, what they'd soon lose. He wanted it to be a celebration of what they shared. So he pushed aside the struggle in his heart and bent his head to claim her lips again.

"Let it be this," he whispered, and she nodded. "What do you want next?"

She pulled back slightly and stared up at him in the firelight. "What do I want next?"

"If you could have whatever you wanted from me tonight, what would you want next?" he clarified as he traced the line of her jaw with his fingertips. "I am yours to command."

She sat up on her elbows and tilted her head, searching his face with a focused intent. "I'm still shaking from what you just did," she said as she touched him. Not a touch with sensual drive, though any time her hands were on him was certainly that, but gentle. She traced his bare bicep, then threaded her fingers with his. "Will you... lay with me for a moment? Just hold me?"

He nodded. "Of course."

She scooted over, giving him a place beside her. He lay on his back and she cuddled into the crook of his shoulder. He wrapped his arms around her as she rested a hand on his chest.

"I can feel your heart," she whispered.

He didn't respond. He knew, because he knew her just as she knew him, that she wasn't talking about his heartbeat through his chest, though she probably could feel that, considering how she made his pulse leap. She was talking about something deeper than that, something more. She was talking about how they felt, what they both wanted, what burned between them and had burned between them since the first moment he laid eyes on her.

"I feel yours, too," he said, and leaned down to kiss her forehead. She turned her face against his shoulder, and he felt the dampness of tears there. He rolled slightly, putting her on her back and covering her. She stared up at him, tears sparkling there in the glorious green of her eyes.

"Not yet," he whispered. "No sadness yet, Phillipa. Tonight is about this. Us."

She nodded and cleared her throat, wiped her tears. She forced a shaky smile. "You're right. Then I know what I want, Rhys."

"What's that?" he asked.

She slid her hand down his side, cupped his hip. "I want to put my mouth on you."

His eyes widened and he grinned. "I won't argue with that, but I will negotiate."

"Negotiate!" she said, and when she giggled it was genuine. "You never said this was a negotiation."

"Wicked of me, I know. But wait until you hear my terms before you refuse me." He kissed her, hard and fast before he said. "I will let you put your mouth on me—"

"A noble sacrifice," she said, her tone dry as dead leaves.

"—*but* I demand I get to do the same to you. At the same time."

She blinked up at him. "How would…that…work?"

He rolled onto his back, dragging her with him so she covered him. "Well, I lay like this," he said. "And you face that way. And while you suck me until my eyes cross, you sit right here…" He pointed to his mouth. "And I make you shake and grind on my tongue."

For a moment he thought he'd gone too far because her eyes got very wide. For all her teasing about his wicked ways, she wasn't open to such a thing. She was a lady, after all. One who had likely been taught that those sorts of things were dirty, if she'd been taught about them at all.

"That sounds like fun," she said at last, then kissed him quickly before she moved.

She turned and adjusted as she sat on his chest and faced his hard cock. She caught him in hand first, stroking him once, twice, sending a ricochet of powerful sensation through every nerve ending in his body. Then she leaned over him and licked the swollen head. "Is this right?"

He tried to focus as he looked down at the wet pussy situated just out of reach for what he wanted. "Almost," he grunted as he grabbed her thighs and yanked her back toward him, settling her against his mouth. He darted out his tongue and traced her. "Perfect."

She ground back, already reaching for release a second time, and whispered, "Perfect."

And then she devoured him as he devoured her.

~

Pippa had made love to Rhys many times since their arrival in Bath. It had been passionate and wild, it had been sweet and comforting...but it had never been a race, a competition. Now, though, with his expert tongue tracing patterns against her clitoris, she felt his challenge. Who would come first? Who would lose control?

She wanted it to be him. To feel the salty flood of him and know she had swept away his control. But he was so good at what he was doing, sucking relentlessly against her clitoris, then switching to spear her with his tongue, that she feared she would lose herself far before he did.

But then again, even when she lost she won with this man. He never took more than she gave, never held anything over her as punishment or to crow over. He was simply not capable of such cruelty, even in its smallest measure.

She pushed those thoughts away and focused instead on pleasing him. She knew how to do it. She'd made a study of it. She took him into her mouth, as deep as she could without gagging, and swirled her tongue around his length. She knew she affected him when he moaned against her, sending vibrations through her sex that made her twitch. Still, she maintained focus as she withdrew almost entirely and stroked her hand down his length, spreading wetness to his base.

She repeated the action, taking him deep, stroking him nearly from her lips. She swirled her tongue, she sucked. She did every single thing that brought him pleasure, and she felt him quicken beneath her as a result. Of course, he kept tormenting too. The focus of his tongue became her clitoris, and it really wasn't fair because she had already come once. She was sensitive and ready, more than he was.

She might have argued that point if her mouth weren't full. So on they went, trying to find the pleasure point that would win the day, trying to force the other's hand. She felt the pleasure building in her. She tried so hard not to surrender to it, not when his legs had begun to shake and she knew he was close.

But in the end, there was nothing to be done. She came, slamming against his mouth as she threw back her head and called out his name in the quiet. He caught her hips, forcing her to grind against his face, to take more pleasure than she thought was possible, and just as the wave of sensation subsided a fraction, he shifted her off him, moved behind her and speared her with his cock in one, long thrust.

She gripped the wrinkled coverlet with both hands as she slammed back against him.

"Oh yes," he grunted. "God, I want to stay like this forever."

"Do it," she whimpered. "We'll never leave this room or this bed. Please, please."

He curled himself around her from behind, cupping her breasts with both hands as he thrust again. She met him and they ground together, finding the rhythm that pleased them both, slow at first, building faster, faster, until their sweat merged and their panting breaths were the only sound in the quiet room.

He caught her hand, braced on the bed, and pushed it between her legs, pressing her fingers there. She rocked against their intertwined hands, seeking pleasure one last shattering time. And only when she came did he slap against her a few more times and then withdraw, the slick heat of his release splashing against her thighs as he came.

She collapsed forward and he fell beside her, pulling her back tight to his chest, their heads at the foot of the bed and their legs tangled near the pillows. For a while, it was quiet, and she reveled in the warmth of his arms around her, the slow calming of his breath against her neck, the pure comfort of just having him here.

And yet she knew it couldn't last. They had made love a long time. It was late. Late enough that he'd probably need to return to his own bed so they wouldn't be caught. She felt him shift, felt him starting to pull away.

She rolled to face him, and they stared at each other in the gathering dark of the dying fire. He touched her cheeks and she felt the tears that had sprung to her eyes returning. She blinked them away. She'd have plenty of time for them later—she didn't want them right now.

He smiled as he kissed her lips, then her cheek, then her forehead. "I wish I could stay with you."

"But you can't," she said. "I know."

He kissed her again and then got up. When his robe was retied, he faced her. She tugged the sheets up around her body and sighed. "I-I know things will change in London, Rhys."

His smile fell slowly. "Phillipa—"

"I'm not trying to ruin this night," she said swiftly. "But this may be the last time we get to be truly alone, and I have to say this."

He nodded, but the action was jerky, forced. "Say whatever you need to say."

"We never made promises," she said. "We both knew we couldn't keep them. We both knew this was a stolen moment in time, that it couldn't last. And tomorrow we'll arrive in the city, where the scandal is at its peak. I know you're going to have a great deal to do to salvage what you can of your own life. And I want you to know that I understand."

He was staring at her, unmoving, unspeaking. For the first time in a very long time, she couldn't read him. Was he relieved? Sorry?

Angry? Sick? Who knew when he had his lord of the manor expression, inscrutable and distant?

She shifted slightly and continued, "I also want to give you my promise that I'll never make it uncomfortable for you. We'll have to see each other regularly because of Kenley. I will be at your service and I'll never behave in a way that will make things difficult."

He was still silent, his hands clenched at his sides.

"Please say something," she whispered.

She held her breath as he ran a hand through his hair. She knew he loved her, even if he never said it. And perhaps there was some part of her that hoped he would. That he would declare himself and that he didn't care what happened next, that he only wanted to be with her.

A fairytale. A children's story. But one she wished could come true.

Instead, he stepped forward and cupped her cheeks. He kissed her, slow and deep and for what felt like forever. When he pulled away, he rested his forehead on hers. "Do you regret it?"

She caught her breath at the very idea. "No," she whispered. "I will never regret it, Rhys. On the contrary, it will sustain me in the years to come."

"As it will me," he whispered. He kissed her once more. She clung to his forearms as he did so, memorizing the feel and the taste of him because she realized this was the last time. It put a crater in her heart, but she managed to keep the truth from her eyes as he released her and backed away.

"Goodbye," he said at the door as he gave her one last look. Then he departed and she was alone.

Goodbye. He'd chosen that word on purpose, she knew. They'd see each other in the morning and many more mornings to come. But it wouldn't be the same. It would never be the same.

And as that realization ravaged her, she sank down on the bed, his scent still lingering in the sheets and on her body, and cried.

CHAPTER 16

P ippa's cheeks hurt from holding the false smile as the carriage turned onto the circular drive of Abigail's London house. It had been a very long day, thanks to her exhaustion after little sleep the night before and the distance that hung between her and Rhys now. He had ridden the entire day on his horse, never joining her in the carriage. At their break for luncheon earlier in the day, he had sat with Kenley and Mr. Barton.

Their goodbye the night before had clearly been painful for them both, but he was moving on. And she knew it was time for her to do the same. But God's teeth, did it hurt like the devil.

The carriage stopped and she drew a breath to calm herself as she waited for the footman to open the door and help her out. Kenley squealed, the high-pitched sound ringing in her ears as she bounced in hopes of soothing him. "Yes, it's been a difficult time. You've been so good, though."

That, of course, did nothing, and when the door to the carriage opened, all on the drive were treated to a squawk that turned into a scream, fun that turned to frustration as quickly as one could say "naptime."

The footman helped her down and she looked up toward the

house. Abigail was standing at the bottom of the steps, Rhys had already swung from his horse and joined her, and with them were Owen and Celeste. All were watching her and as she stepped toward them, Celeste came rushing forward.

"Oh, the baby!" she cooed. "Isn't he precious?"

Kenley stopped screaming and turned his face into Pippa's shoulder, and she smiled as Celeste leaned in to kiss her cheek. "A long day has not made our friend here very amenable to new acquaintances."

"Of course," Celeste said with a broad smile as she stepped back to Owen and tossed him a hard stare.

There was no misreading its intent. Clearly Celeste was already planning ahead for her own family. And Owen didn't look opposed to the idea. For a brief moment, the two of them were locked together, wordless communication flowing between them, and Pippa couldn't deny that she was jealous.

She wanted Celeste to be happy, but knowing she never could be...well, that made it hard to see.

She looked toward the man himself and then slid her gaze away as Abigail stepped toward her, expression gentle. "Welcome home, love. Well, home for a little while at any rate."

Rhys cleared his throat. "Yes, I do apologize. The home my solicitor selected will be perfect for you, but it required a repair we did not anticipate. I'm assured it will be fully ready in less than a week's time. Mr. and Mrs. Barton were kind enough to take the other carriage on ahead so they can fully prepare the place for your arrival."

"And you offered me a place here," Pippa said. "And I'm forever grateful. Though this screaming child may change your mind."

As she said it, Nan stepped forward and held out her arms for Kenley. "Let me take him, ma'am. I'll change him and get him to sleep, and I'm sure he'll be right as rain in a few hours."

Pippa handed the boy over gratefully, and Abigail signaled for a servant to escort Nan to the chamber for Kenley. "I've had adjoining rooms prepared for you and young Master Kenley, if that is all right with you."

"Yes," Pippa said. "Though Nan may end up being his nursemaid, I certainly want to be close to him."

Rhys wrinkled his brow. "You want Nan as his nursemaid?"

She pressed her lips together. "Yes, I spoke to her about it in the carriage after lunch."

He was quiet a moment, and then he inclined his head. "A very good choice. I suppose we will hire a new maid for you, then."

She shook her head. "I am under your employ now, I think, my lord. I will no longer require a maid—I will make do for myself."

He shifted slightly and the silence that hung between them must have been uncomfortable because Abigail slipped her arm into the crook of Pippa's and squeezed gently. "Come in, won't you both? I have a tea laid out with some wonderful delicacies and we'd love to chat with you."

Rhys cleared his throat and shook his head. "I greatly appreciate it, Abigail, but I have much to do. I think I'll walk home and stretch my legs before I get to it. Good afternoon to you all."

He pivoted, his eyes remaining on Pippa for a moment too long before they were forced away. Then he stepped off, said a few words to the footman, apparently about his horse, if his gestures were of any indication.

Pippa stared after him, wishing tears didn't fill her eyes again. Blinking at them as if she could will them not to fall.

Owen glanced at Celeste, and then he said, "I think I'll follow him. I have something to discuss with him."

He bounded off down the steps, leaving Abigail and Celeste behind. The three Mrs. Montgomerys stared at each other, much as they had the first time they'd met here weeks before. Only this time Pippa knew them both so well. She counted them as friends.

And she couldn't hide her broken heart as she bent her head. Abigail and Celeste made twin sounds of distress as they hurried to her, and suddenly she was enveloped by them both. She let them buoy her up, guide her into the house.

"This is so silly," she whispered.

Abigail shook her head as they led her to the front parlor where the tea was spread out in waiting. "No it isn't," she insisted, smiling as Celeste took Pippa to the settee where they sat together. "Not in the slightest. Would you like something to eat or drink?"

"Perhaps in a moment," Pippa said. "After I've gathered myself a little and not sniveling like a ninny."

"Please, you aren't sniveling," Celeste said with a laugh. "But we can see how troubled you are. Oh, Pippa, what happened in Bath?"

Pippa worried her lip and stared at her clasped hands on her lap. Abigail took the seat on the other side of her and her two friends waited, very quietly, very patiently…though Pippa had no doubt she wasn't going to be allowed to worm her way out of this.

She cleared her throat. "I had a difficult time with my parents upon my arrival. And there were some unpleasant encounters in the town now that the truth about Erasmus and his many wives is out in public."

Her two friends flinched. That was a fact that affected them all.

"I'm certain that was all very unpleasant," Abigail said with a quick glance at Celeste. "But I think you know we're asking about what happened between you and Lord Leighton."

Pippa gasped and jerked her head up to find both her friends staring at her evenly. "I—"

"You don't have to tell us, of course," Celeste assured her with a gentle hand on her knee. "But it's obvious something happened, and we are sisters in this horrific experience, aren't we? No one wants to judge, just help."

"Oh, I know you wouldn't judge," Pippa said softly. "Though I would deserve it."

They waited for her, letting her consider her next move. Truth be told, she so desperately wanted to reveal everything to them. She needed to say it all out loud, to pour it out because maybe it wouldn't fester so much. Perhaps if she heard it out loud, she could find some way to fight it.

She took a long breath and let it fall from her lips. That she was in love with him. That she believed him in love with her, too. That they'd become lovers. And that it was over, which was why the tension had flowed between them today. When she was finished, she felt the tear slide down her cheek and hated herself for it.

But neither of her friends seemed to feel that way. Abigail put her arms around her and drew her closer, letting Pippa rest a head on her shoulder. "You two always had a deeper connection," she said softly. "From the first moment he and Mr. Gregory arrived with you at the beginning of this madness, I saw the spark."

"I will never forget when he came to the boarding house where I was staying while I searched for Erasmus. When Rhys walked in, it was like someone turned me inside out," Pippa admitted. "I could hardly breathe. I hated myself for being so weak, and hated myself more when I realized the earl was Erasmus's brother. How unseemly! How dreadful and wrong."

"No, it isn't," Celeste said with a sharp shake of her head. "There is nothing wrong with any of us looking for love where we can find it. Erasmus was a great many horrible things, but his brother has never been anything but decent. And he's handsome, too. Are you certain there is nothing that can be done about it?"

"Of course not," Pippa said, getting to her feet and pacing the room. "We all know the situation. Rhys has a legacy to protect, a name and a title to rebuild. If he linked himself to me...even as a mere mistress...it would send ripples through Society that he would likely never recover from." She sighed. "I-I wouldn't do that to him. I love him too much."

"Oh, Pippa," Abigail whispered.

"Please don't feel pity," Pippa said. "I couldn't bear it, and I must be able to bear so much more. I will take on a role helping to raise Kenley. Rhys wants to be a part of his life, too, to help him be prepared for whatever will come. I must find a way to let go of this.

To bury it, even if I cannot kill it. So if I look at you two and see pity every time I mention Rhys's name or am in the same room as the man…"

"I understand," Celeste said. "You will have no pity from us, love. I promise. Only support."

"Yes," Abigail said, but a little slower. "Always our support." She worried her lip. "So how was it, though?"

Celeste's mouth dropped open and she pivoted toward her friend. "Abigail!"

"Please, as if you weren't wondering the same thing." Abigail snorted.

Celeste opened and shut her mouth like a fish, but her cheeks filled with color that proved Abigail's point. With anyone else in the world, Pippa would have rebuffed the wildly inappropriate question, but here? Here she could be honest.

She moved toward them, clasping her hands to her chest. "I had no idea it could be like that. The man is…*magical.*"

"Excellent," Abigail said, casting a quick glance toward Celeste. "You deserve nothing less. Though I suppose our Celeste wins the prize, for she married her gentleman."

Celeste blushed bright as a plum. "You two!" she gasped.

Pippa laughed and the cheeky comment seemed to lighten the entire room. All of them moved to the sideboard to get tea. But even as she tried to return to some kind of normalcy with her friends, Pippa couldn't help but think of the man who had left her side less than half an hour before.

And know that things would never be the same again, and the rest of her life would only be pretending that was acceptable.

Rhys bent his head and kept his gaze focused on the path before him. The park across from Abigail's house created an excellent short cut to his home, though he wasn't thinking about home or anything he had to do. He only had one thought: Pippa.

"Leighton!"

He snapped his head up at the sound of his name being called from behind him. He turned and saw Owen Gregory rushing up behind him. His heart sank. He was not in the mood to talk, even with a man he'd come to consider a friend. Gregory was too good an investigator not to see all the things Rhys wished to conceal. But there was no way to avoid the encounter, so he stopped and stepped off the path so Gregory could catch up.

"I didn't hear you there," Rhys said.

"I know," Owen panted. "I've been following you for some time, saying your name."

"Ah." Rhys shook his head. "Woolgathering, I suppose."

"I know you have a great deal on your mind," Gregory said. "Were you able to take care of everything in Bath?"

Rhys pursed his lips and tried not to think of making love to Phillipa. Of the bonds they had formed there and how much they mattered. If he thought too hard about it, Gregory would see. Perhaps he'd never bring it up, but he would know.

"I think I managed," Rhys said carefully. "Though with my brother, one can never be certain. The solicitor I hired believed he uncovered all the debts and issues and I resolved them."

Gregory's expression softened. "I am very sorry. I'm sure that wasn't easy. But now that you are back in London, at least I can help you."

Rhys snorted. "I'm not sure I can afford you anymore, Owen."

Gregory lifted his eyebrows at the unexpected informality, but didn't correct Rhys. "I wasn't offering as an employee, *Rhys*."

Rhys stared at him, this man who had been the bearer of bad news and was now offering to be a...friend, he supposed. And Rhys had few enough of those, even fewer thanks to the scandal.

"I would appreciate that," he said softly. "Thank you."

"I've been following up on Rosie Stanton while you were away," Gregory said.

"Kenley's mother," Rhys said. "This never ends. Yes, I know before I left that there were rumors she had gotten on a ship, heading to America. Did that pan out?"

"She was seen on the docks; she inquired about passage twice, once to Maryland, again to Lower Canada, but…" Gregory held his gaze. "There is no evidence she actually boarded either ship."

Rhys wrinkled his brow. "Why not? She murdered a man, and though it's been covered up as an accident now, she must still fear the consequences. Why wouldn't she start a new life?"

"One can only assume it is the attachment to her child that keeps her here," Gregory said. "My larger concern is why she made such a public display of potentially leaving. It might be she simply changed her mind. But she could be trying to leave a trail that convinces us… convinces *you*…that she's left when she'd really still here."

Rhys's stomach turned. "If it was done with that kind of subterfuge in mind, that is troubling, indeed." He thought of Kenley and Phillipa, who would ultimately be the target of the woman if she had revenge or recovery in mind. "Can you subtly put guards on Abigail's house?" he asked.

"I will make the arrangements," Gregory said. "But shouldn't you tell Pippa? And the others?"

Rhys nodded. "I should. And I will, but I'd like to wait until I know a little more. Until I'm more certain. Phillipa is…it's difficult enough for her without adding what might be unwarranted fear to the mix."

Gregory's gaze held Rhys's evenly. "I see."

"I'm sure you do. It's an annoying habit of yours. But I don't wish to talk about it, not now at any rate."

"It might help," Gregory said softly.

"Yes, I suppose it might. But for right now, I want to just wallow in my misery. Feeling the pain lets me recall that there is something else to feel. Something worth the agony." Rhys reached out a hand

and Gregory shook it firmly. "Thank you for your help and for your friendship. I might not deserve it, but I appreciate it nonetheless."

"You deserve it," Gregory said. "And you shall always have it. Now I should return to my wife. I'll have a guard on the house before sundown."

Rhys inclined his head. "Again, thank you."

He turned on his heel and walked away from his friend, but with every step his entire body felt heavier. This discussion was a stark reminder that his future had been torn apart by his brother's behavior. A reminder that all the dreams he might have once had would have to be set aside, along with the woman he was leaving behind at Abigail's home.

CHAPTER 17

The three days since her return to London had been far busier than Pippa had imagined they would be. Abigail and Celeste kept her entertained, she thought as a distraction from her troubles. She couldn't deny it was wonderful reconnecting with them both.

Occasionally Mrs. Barton arrived with swatches and sketches so Pippa could make decisions about items and decorations for the new house. Kenley had settled in and was back to his usually bubbly and happy self. He was a great favorite of both her friends and everyone in Abigail's staff.

It should have been a very full and exciting time. And yet she was not happy. Even now she stood at the window of her chamber, staring out at the garden below, and her thoughts turned to Rhys.

She had not seen him since he left her the afternoon of her arrival in the city. He hadn't called, he hadn't written. She was too afraid to ask about him, though she guessed he might be calling on Owen Gregory, so Celeste might see him. Still, her friend never brought the subject up. A kindness, of course, but all of it left Pippa feeling…so empty. In the time they'd spent in Bath, she'd become accustomed to seeing Rhys's face at her table each morning. She was used to being able to talk to him about her problems, or Kenley, or the weather.

And at night…well, the night was the worst part. Her bed felt huge, and she found herself reaching across to see if he was there. To see if he had joined her somehow. She ached for him, and she woke up wet and shaking from dreams of his hands on her, his mouth on her.

And yet she was always alone.

"This will fade," she said softly, pressing her hand to the cool glass. "Time will dull the sting."

She said the words, but it was hard to believe them at present. It was all a *hope* that the empty feeling would go away.

"Mrs. Montgomery?" Pippa turned to find one of Abigail's maids at the door. "Mrs. Montgomery asks that you join her for tea."

Pippa nodded. The poor servants were still tripping over themselves to figure out what to call all these wives of a liar. At least Celeste had a new name, so that made it easier. Still, it was time to think about if she wanted to go back to being Pippa Windridge. God, if her father heard about that…

"Ma'am?"

She jolted as she realized she had spiraled off into thought without answering the poor young woman waiting for her. "Of course. I'll be down straight away."

As the servant left, Pippa went to the mirror and smoothed a hand over her hair. With Nan taking over nursemaid duties for Kenley, Pippa had begun doing her own preparations in the morning. Not that difficult, as she had done so for months while Rosie Stanton was off incubating a baby for Erasmus.

"No time to be bitter," Pippa muttered as she left the room and went down the long hallway. She came down the stairs, trying to gather her tangled thoughts. As she came into the parlor where she and Abigail always shared tea, she said, "You know, it might be a very good day to take Kenley to the park. The weather is still—"

She cut herself off because as she entered the room, she realized

Abigail wasn't alone. Rhys stood at the fireplace, his face pale as he watched her enter the chamber. They stared at each other for a moment. God, but he was handsome. More than she remembered in those heated dreams. And all she wanted to do was cross the room and cup his cheeks. She wanted to pull his mouth to hers and drown in him.

She had been wrong when she thought these feelings might go away with time. They would never go away. She saw the long line of her future stretch out before her and she knew, with complete certainty, that every time she saw this man, it would be like this. It would hurt more, not less, as he eventually moved on. Married. Had children with some other woman. It would only get worse.

"Lord Leighton has joined us," Abigail said from the sideboard where she was pouring tea. "Though you've obviously noticed that."

Pippa shot her friend a glare. Abigail had arranged this, clearly, and not told her about it. To surprise her. To keep her from finding some way of getting out of seeing Rhys.

"Lord Leighton," she said, and wished her voice wasn't so breathless.

"Mrs...Miss..." He dipped his head. "Phillipa."

Her knees went weak when he said her name. Damn him. She fought the response and moved to help Abigail with the tea.

"Why?" she hissed out between clenched teeth.

Abigail ignored her and handed her a cup. "Take this to our guest, won't you, dear?"

Nostrils flaring, Pippa took the cup and brought it to Rhys. His fingers brushed hers as he took it, and she sucked in a breath and nearly dumped the entire thing on him when she snatched her hand away.

"I wanted to get an update from Rhys about all that's been going on," Abigail said, motioning for them to sit together on the settee while she took the chair by the fire across from them.

Pippa pursed her lips. Abigail went too far—Pippa was going to have to have words with her later. Still, she took the seat beside

Rhys, trying not to let her knees touch his even though he filled the settee with his ridiculous, masculine, wonderful presence.

He cleared his throat and took a sip of tea before he responded. "I'm not sure what updates there are to share. I'm making final arrangements to pay off the debts on this home so that it may be turned over to you, Abigail."

Pippa glanced at Abigail. At least in this she could be happy. "I'm so glad you're retaining the house."

Abigail smiled. "I've told Rhys several times that it's too extravagant a gift to make, especially since he is also settling with me financially, but he is, as I think you know, insistent."

Rhys set his cup down and ran a hand through his hair, the way he always did when he was uncomfortable. "My brother should have made these arrangements for his wife."

"Yes, but which one?" Abigail asked with a little laugh. "I'm sure he must have been very confused with all of us plus any other lovers he was collecting on the side."

Rhys's mouth thinned and he looked away, almost as if he felt guilty. "Well, it falls to me to take care of all of that. The house was gifted to my brother upon our father's death. That he borrowed against it to finance all his misdeeds should not affect you. So it will be passed to you as it always should have been. And the allowance is also standard. You must be able to live."

Pippa felt his anxiety about this topic. She knew what a strain all these arrangements put on him. And yet he did it, without complaint, without hesitation. He took responsibility for something that was not his fault and made amends in ways that would not help him in the future. Because it was right.

Abigail seemed equally as struck, and she smiled at him. "You are too good, Lord Leighton." She glanced at Pippa, made no effort to hide the look, and then said, "You know, I have forgotten an arrangement I need to make with my staff. Will you two excuse me for a moment?"

She didn't wait for the response, but swept from the room, shutting the door behind her. Pippa caught her breath and glanced at Rhys.

"She is not very subtle, is she?" he asked with a half-smile.

She shook her head. "No," she laughed, though she felt suddenly nervous. "She is never that."

"She's guessed...something happened between us?" he asked.

She couldn't tell by his tone what he thought of that, but guilt rippled through her regardless. She had been imprudent in sharing the truth, even if it was just to her friends. Even if saying out loud how she felt and what she'd done had released a pressure valve.

"They are...intelligent," she said. "And have eyes."

He nodded. "Yes. I think Owen Gregory guessed something as well. I suppose we aren't good at hiding it."

She bent her head. "We will have to become better at it."

There was a long silence, and she felt his gaze boring into her. Then he sighed. "You look beautiful, Phillipa. Like a dream."

He stepped toward her and took her hand, letting his thumb stroke over her skin. She shivered as she lifted her eyes to him. There was no denying the intensity in his stare.

"We must fight this, mustn't we?" she asked, the tone of her voice too breathy. "As much as we don't want to."

"I know you're correct," he said, but didn't release her. "I want to care about that. But I miss you."

She caught her breath at that admission, softly given but as powerful as a blast to the chest. "Rhys," she whispered as she backed away. It took every ounce of strength to do it.

"I'm sorry," he said, smoothing his jacket. "That wasn't fair, to either of us."

"Well, nothing in this situation is fair," she said. "That isn't your fault or mine."

"How is Kenley?"

She smiled at the change of subject, for at least the boy gave her no difficult emotions. "Very well. He likes Abigail a great deal, and he is adjusting nicely to having Nan as a nursemaid, but I think he does miss you."

He pursed his lips. "I've not done a very good job in checking in and that isn't fair to him. I'll make a schedule to see him more regularly."

Leave it to Rhys to find a way to plan his way out of trouble. She did like that side of him: the planner. The fixer. "I'm sure that will help, especially when we move to the new house. He will have an adjustment period and friendly faces will be a comfort."

Rhys shifted and his gaze darted away, but not before she saw worry on his face. Something that went deeper than the connection to her. Deeper, even, than whatever hesitations he had regarding Kenley's future.

"What is it?" she asked.

He drew in a long breath. "Rosie Stanton has not left London."

All her tangled thoughts about Rhys fled her mind as fear replaced them. She remembered Rosie's angry face when Pippa, Abigail and Celeste had gone to confront her. How she'd been part of holding Celeste at gunpoint. She remembered the moment when Rosie had shot Erasmus. That twisted rage that had made her pretty features terrifying.

She stared at him. "Wh-what?"

He moved closer. "You're pale. Sit."

She did as he asked, and he rejoined her on the settee. "Please tell me what is going on," she whispered.

"We thought she had left the country on a ship bound for Maryland."

"Yes, I recall that before we left for Bath weeks ago. Are you saying she didn't?"

"Owen found out that she had inquired about a boat to America and another to Lower Canada…but she took neither. She seems to have disappeared back into her old life here in the city."

Pippa could hardly hear over the beating of her heart now. "I… why would she do that when she has so much to lose?" He stared at her evenly, and she slid away from him, as if moving back would erase what she understood. "Kenley."

He nodded. "The day she shot my brother she made it clear how much she loved the boy."

"Erasmus wanted to abandon him and it enraged her. No matter what else she's done, I know she cares deeply and genuinely for her child," Pippa breathed. "But that doesn't change the fact that she was complicit in a slew of Erasmus's bad deeds."

"And that she killed him," Rhys added softly.

She heard the lingering pain in his voice. She reached for his hand, but then stopped herself. They'd begun this situation saying they had to become better at hiding their connection. No matter what she wanted, she had to make that effort. She forced her hand back into her lap.

"Yes, also that she killed him." Pippa tried to focus, to think about what rational step needed to be taken next. "I would be more comfortable if we had a guard on the house. If Rosie maintains an interest in the child, we need someone watching for her so we aren't surprised by anything she does."

He did what she had stopped herself from doing and caught her hand. "It's done, Pippa. Someone has been watching over you for a few days now and they'll continue to do so until we have surmised what Miss Stanton may want."

She stared at him as understanding dawned and slowly pulled her hand from his. "Someone has been watching the house for *days*?"

"Since our return in London," he said. "Why?"

"You…you knew this threat existed and you didn't tell me?" She stood up and backed away.

He watched her go, his cheeks paling. "Phillipa—"

"Why didn't you tell me immediately?"

He let out what sounded like an exhausted sigh before he got up. "There was so much going on, so much for you to worry about as you arrived in London and settled yourself and Kenley."

She stepped toward him, fisting her hands at her sides. "You brought me back to London *for* Kenley. My *duty* is to watch out for that child, and if I don't know all the details, any of the details, about a potential threat against him, I cannot do that. I can't protect him. What if she had gotten past your guard, Rhys? I would have had no idea that was even a possibility—"

He shook his head and interrupted her. "First off, I did not bring you to London merely for Kenley, and you know that."

Those words stunned her into silence. They meant too much. She folded her arms and stared at him as he continued, "And I see now that yes, it was a mistake to keep you in the dark. I apologize. Truly, I was only thinking of your well-being. I didn't want to upset you. I didn't want Rosie Stanton coming back to haunt you. Not after what she did to you."

Pippa blinked at the passion in his voice. At the sweetness of his misguided actions. How could they make her so angry and also make her want to kiss him?

But no, she couldn't think about that. "You are not responsible for me," she said softly. "I am not some delicate flower you must protect."

"But I *wanted* to protect you," he snapped, and his blue eyes were as dark as stormy seas.

"And I am..." She swallowed hard because the next part was so painful. "I am not your problem, Rhys. Lord Leighton. I never was."

His lips pressed together hard, but he didn't argue with her. How could he? They both knew what was happening, they were both adults.

"I should go...check on him," she said. "Please send me the particulars regarding Miss Stanton and this guard of yours. I'd like to meet him, and I will write to you and let you know if I find him satisfactory."

He choked out a laugh at that, but there was no humor to it, only pain. "I see. We are to correspond through letters alone then?"

She nodded. "That might be best for a while, considering. To limit our contact only to the child."

"Don't do this," he whispered.

Tears filled her eyes and she drew a few breaths to calm herself so they wouldn't fall. "I must. Your desire to protect me must not supersede your drive to protect him...or yourself." She stepped away from him to the door of the chamber. "Time will make these feelings fade, my lord. It must. And when they have, then we can be friends again. We can forget that there was ever something more. Good day."

She left him, rushing down the hall, hands shaking. She passed Abigail on her way to the stairs and her friend said her name, but she ignored it as she rushed up and headed toward Kenley's room.

She'd been a fool to forget herself, but she could fix that. Even if she didn't believe her parting words to Rhys one bit. Even if she knew that what she felt wouldn't alter, no matter how much time passed, no matter how much she tried to make it go away.

CHAPTER 18

R hys pivoted away from the door as Phillipa made her exit, and moved to the window. It looked down over the street, over the park across the way. He saw none of it because everything in his heart and soul and body was focused on the fact that she had found the strength he couldn't. She had walked away, and it felt so permanent.

He slapped a palm against the window with a growl of pure pain and bent his head. Damn his brother for bringing all this destruction down on everyone in his life. Damn him for hurting Phillipa. And for creating a situation where Rhys could never have her.

"Rhys, are you well?"

He jumped and turned to find Abigail standing in the parlor door, watching him with concern in her brown eyes. He fought to maintain some dignity, to smile and play this all off. But he had no energy for it. "Leave it alone, Abigail," he said.

Her expression shifted and she stepped forward. "Rhys—"

"Leave it alone," he repeated, this time harsher, louder, and he hated himself for losing control that way, but now the box was open and he couldn't stuff everything back inside. "I'm well aware that you know something about what happened between Phillipa and me in Bath. I'm certain you think that gives you the right to meddle, as you did this afternoon. But I beg of you to leave it be."

Her lips parted and he saw...*pity* in her eyes. He supposed he ought to become accustomed to such an expression. Anyone who looked at him anymore either did so with pity or contempt. Except Phillipa. And now he'd lost her.

"I understand why you don't wish to speak to me about it," Abigail said, and her tone was gentle, as if she were speaking to a child not much older than Kenley. "Rhys, you are tormenting yourself over Phillipa and everything else. It cannot be healthy to hold all that inside and try to pretend you are strong enough to carry it by yourself."

"Well, the person I would discuss it with just left me here in the parlor, didn't she?" he said, throwing up his hands. "So what would you have me do, Abigail? Open a vein in the park across the street so the world can see me bleed?"

"Of course not." She edged closer. "I cannot believe I'm about to suggest this, considering he is the most infuriating man in London —nay, the entire country—but won't you consider going to the Duke of Gilmore?"

Rhys shut his eyes. "Gilmore is not in Town."

"He returns tomorrow morning, though," Abigail said. "And he is your friend, Rhys. You need one of those."

Rhys looked at her and pondered asking her why she knew the comings and goings of Gilmore, a man she had said more than once that she despised. But he was too tired to do so. And she wasn't wrong that he needed to pour himself out to someone who cared. Someone who wouldn't judge.

Much.

Abigail stepped closer yet again. "I...I meddled today, thinking it would be harmless, but I can see that it wasn't. I'm sorry."

He shook his head. "It is I who should be sorry. I am not in good spirits, but you don't deserve my ire."

"No, a man dead in the grave deserves it," Abigail said with a shrug. "But since none of us can make him pay more for his crimes than he already is, we must be a bit more understanding with each other. If you trespassed, you are certainly forgiven."

"Thank you," he said, and meant it. "Now I must go. I can't be here any longer."

She stepped aside to allow him to depart, and he did so with just a wave goodbye to her. He burst from her home and crossed the street for the short walk across the park, then a few streets more to his home.

But with every step, his body, mind and heart felt all the heavier. And all that he'd lost thanks to Erasmus became so much harder to accept.

～

P ippa was still in a fog when she trudged down the stairs for supper later that night. She hadn't wanted to join Abigail, but to stay in Kenley's room, watching over him as if the hounds of hell were about to descend at any moment.

No, not hounds. The child's mother. A woman who had every right to him, as Pippa didn't. A woman who could also be a threat to the boy. So what was right? What was best?

She shook her head. She would have stayed at his side, watching him play, watching him sleep, but the invitation from Abigail had not seemed to be one she could refuse. She entered the dining room and found that Abigail was not there, but Celeste was.

"Good evening," Pippa said as she crossed the room to her. "I didn't expect you tonight."

"Abigail called for me to join you," Celeste said as she kissed her cheek. When she pulled away, Pippa felt her concerned gaze. "How are you?"

"Abigail has been talking," Pippa said with a sigh.

Abigail had seen her hasty retreat from Rhys earlier in the day, of course, but she had never said a word about it to Pippa. In fact, her friend had left her alone all afternoon, until the demands to be joined for supper. Pippa had thought she'd escaped the scrutiny, but it appeared Abigail was only waiting for back up.

"Only because we're worried about you." They turned together as Abigail entered the room. She crossed to take Pippa's hand and gave it a brief, comforting squeeze. "Only because I care."

As Abigail released her, Pippa sank into her place at the table and the others joined her. She sighed again. "I realize your interference is kindly meant. I do. But there is nothing anyone can do, and certainly you both have other things to do. Celeste, you are mere weeks into a marriage—ought you not to be spending every waking moment with your doting husband?"

Celeste blushed slightly. "I spend most moments with him, I assure you. Mustn't one get out for fresh air? Besides, I like that he misses me."

Her happiness was so plain that Pippa couldn't help but smile, and it lightened the load she carried a little. She shifted her attention to Abigail. "And you have your own problems to attend to, don't you?"

Abigail snorted out a laugh before she took a long drink from her glass of wine. "I got hissed out of a shop today, so I suppose I should say yes. But focusing on your problems seems so much less hideous."

"Hissed out of a shop?" Pippa said, leaning forward.

Abigail shrugged. "We all know the scandal that was created. None of us are fools, are we?"

Celeste sighed. "I am sorry. It is abominably cruel that anyone would blame the victims of a crime rather than the criminal."

"They would blame him, were he not dead," Abigail said with a dry laugh. "Unfortunately, all that's left is us and his poor brother."

Pippa squeezed her eyes shut as she thought of Rhys and his exhausted expression earlier that day. At the pain in his voice back in Bath, when he told her about the estrangement that had started long before Erasmus's bad deeds. He had lost so much. It had bonded them for a time.

"Do you want to talk about what happened between you and the earl this afternoon?" Abigail pressed.

"There is nothing to talk about." That wasn't true, but Pippa *couldn't* say the rest. "As you say, Lord Leighton is being maligned for his brother's actions even more deeply than we are. I've simply realized that the best thing I can do if I…if I care for him is to let him go. He does not need my presence in his life, creating even more trouble."

"Pippa," Celeste breathed.

She held up a hand. "Oh, please don't. If I talk about it, I'll break down, and I can't do that right now. Perhaps later, later when things are more settled, then I'll have myself a good old-fashioned collapse."

Abigail worried her lip. "Everything in me tells me to push and prod and be the nuisance the Duke of Gilmore always says I am. But I will try to respect your wishes in this, Pippa."

"Thank you."

The first course was brought out and they all began to eat. As they talked about everything and nothing all at once, Pippa observed her friends. Both were so clever, and aside from Rhys, they were the only people in the world who could understand what she was experiencing.

And perhaps if she couldn't talk to them about the complicated situation with Rhys, she could request their assistance on another score.

When the dessert was placed before them, Pippa did not pick up her fork. Instead she said, "You said earlier that you wished to help me."

Abigail straightened immediately. "Yes! Are you ready to discuss whatever happened earlier today?"

"Gracious, Abigail, you *are* pushing," Celeste whispered, as if Pippa couldn't hear her just as plainly as Abigail did.

She smiled despite the seriousness of the situation. She did adore these two women. "It isn't about Rhys. No one can do anything about Rhys, not even me."

Abigail opened her mouth as if to protest, but Pippa held up a hand with a laugh. "Please stop, I can read your thoughts—I don't need you to say them and start this conversation all over again."

"What do you need help with?" Celeste asked with another hard look at Abigail.

"Kenley," Pippa said, and the laughter faded from her voice because none of what she was about to say was amusing in the slightest. "Rhys told me today that Rosie Stanton did not leave the country as we all believed. She is still in London. And there is reason to believe that might be because of her son."

All the teasing and prodding and playful interaction between the women vanished in an instant. Abigail sat up straighter, Celeste's cheeks went pale. They had all been there the day Rosie shot Erasmus Montgomery. They had all been threatened by the woman in her desperate hour.

"Tell us everything," Celeste said, her voice shaking.

"There isn't much more to say," Pippa said with a sigh. "There was little more I was told, except that Rhys...Lord Leighton...hired a guard to watch over this house a few days ago."

Abigail's brow wrinkled. "There's some man watching over my house?"

"Apparently. I asked Lord Leighton to give me the particulars so that I could ascertain if this person is an acceptable guard," Pippa said.

Abigail arched a brow. "I'm sure that went well."

"I surprised him, I'm sure."

"You needn't keep calling him Lord Leighton, not in front of us," Celeste said softly.

Pippa bowed her head. "I have to practice doing so. Calling him by his first name was always too familiar. I need to start distancing myself and this is a step in that process. I wish I could stop *thinking* about him as Rhys. That will be much harder."

"Oh, dearest," Abigail said, and caught her hand. "Are you certain you don't want to talk more about it?"

"I'm certain," Pippa said. "I must be certain. And I must focus on Rosie now, and what she might want from Kenley. The guard is fine, of course. I hope his presence will keep the child safe, but I don't know. Rosie is wily and resourceful, duplicitous and sly. It took me a long time to realize she was my husband's lover when they were under my very nose. She's certainly the sort of person who could subvert any security measures even the Earl of Leighton put in place."

"You want to do something about it?" Abigail said.

Pippa nodded. "I think I...*we*...should perhaps try to find her ourselves."

Celeste pushed from the table and backed away. "She and Erasmus worked together not just to deceive you, but to fake his death. She was part of his final plan to kill us all. To frame Abigail for a murder that didn't happen. How can you want to seek such a person out?"

"But for Erasmus, I don't know that she would have hatched such a plan herself," Pippa said. "Certainly she turned her ire on him quickly enough, which shows she questioned what he desired. But I understand your hesitation, Celeste. He put the gun in your back. And you have so much to lose. If you don't want to be part of my scheme—we'll call it what it is, a scheme—I understand."

"Surely Rhys and Owen are already looking into this themselves," Abigail suggested, even as she got up and slid her arm around Celeste to comfort her. "Don't you trust them to take care of it?"

"I do, completely," Pippa said. "But I don't trust that Rosie would allow herself to be caught by them."

"And why would she allow *us* to catch her?" Celeste asked. "There is no love lost between us."

"No, but in her heart, she must know that we share a bond. She was a victim of Erasmus as well as an accomplice. If we reach out, she might believe she has more sympathy, especially if we do it right. I doubt there is any chance she feels that would happen if she spoke to Rhys."

Abigail pursed her lips as she and Celeste exchanged a look. "That's a good point," Abigail said.

Pippa gave a small smile. "Excellent. I've been trying to put together a good point for hours, so I'm pleased I succeeded."

Celeste pulled away and paced the room a moment, a troubled expression on her face. Pippa crossed to her and caught her hands. "If this is too much for you, I entirely understand. You don't have to take part in this."

Celeste shook her head. "Owen would be very angry if he found out I was going behind his back."

"Aren't you angry he didn't tell you about Rosie himself?" Pippa asked, thinking again of her encounter with Rhys that afternoon.

"No," Celeste said. "He is well aware of my emotional reaction to the events of a few weeks ago. He comforts me through the nightmares when they come. If he didn't tell me, I know in my heart it was only to protect me. And that he would have told me eventually, when the time was right."

Pippa blinked. What her friend was describing was faith. Absolute faith in the best intentions of a partner, in the strength of a bond that could not be broken by any foolishness. Celeste was lucky to have it. Pippa couldn't threaten it.

"I would feel...better..." she said slowly. "...if someone I trusted in every way was here in the house with Kenley."

"Yes," Abigail said. "That's an excellent idea."

"You don't want me at your side?" Celeste whispered.

"Pippa and I have much less to lose," Abigail clarified. "We love you too much to threaten what you've built. At any rate, you would be helping because you'd be very aware of what dangers existed for Kenley."

"Well, I do like being with him," Celeste said with a small smile. "It allows me to practice for the future, for when Owen and I have our own children."

Pippa smiled. Celeste deserved this happiness, this future. "That settles it then. Abigail and I will do the work on the ground to find Rosie. And Celeste will help us plan and be there for Kenley while we search."

Celeste still seemed uncertain, but she nodded.

"Very good," Abigail said. "And how do you suggest we find Rosie?"

"Well, we know where she stayed before," Pippa said. "And where she worked. We could start there."

Abigail nodded. "I'll get some paper and we can work out some of the details while we finish our dessert."

She left the room, and Pippa and Celeste retook their seats. Celeste was staring at her.

"What do you want to say?" Pippa asked.

Celeste shrugged. "If you manage to connect with Rosie, if you get her to talk to you rather than fight what she fears you'll do… what do you want her to say?"

"I just want to know her…her motivations in staying in London rather than doing what is best for her and leaving. I want to know what she'll do next in regard to Kenley."

"Would you let her see him if that was her desire?"

Pippa swallowed hard. "She's his mother. Does she not have a right to see him? Does he not have a right to know her?"

Celeste pondered that. "It's hard for me to answer, given our history with the woman. I can see how she was used by Erasmus, as everyone in his life was used by him. But I also know she went along with a great many of his crimes."

"Perhaps when I see her, it will be easier to know the answer," Pippa said. "I hope it will be."

Abigail returned to the room, paper and charcoal pencils in hand. She handed out the items, and as they ate their dessert, they did exactly as she'd suggested. They created a plan to find and speak to the woman who had betrayed Phillipa beneath her very nose. The woman who had given her the child she loved more than anything.

Pippa only hoped that by the time she found her, she would know what to do.

CHAPTER 19

R hys was glad he could depend on one thing in his topsy-turvy life: when he called for the Duke of Gilmore, his friend always came. Even when it was directly from the road after his return from Cornwall, where he'd been visiting his sister the last week.

But Gilmore was here now, and as Rhys entered the parlor, the duke got to his feet and smiled. "Good morning."

"Good morning," Rhys said, extending a hand. "Sorry to call you here just as you were arriving home."

Gilmore shrugged. "What's sleep when there are such friends to be had? Though I admit I was surprised to have your missive waiting for me when I arrived this morning. Is everything well?"

"Not at all," Rhys said with a laugh. "I've been banned from my club, invitations to long-planned parties have been rescinded. I would say I have been shunned by about half our social circle."

Gilmore let out his breath in a low whistle. "Christ. That's terrible, Leighton. Is there something I can do? I could speak to Samson and Williams at the club."

Rhys shook his head. "And sully your own good name? The fact you're remaining at my side will do that enough. No, I've had an invitation from Fitzhugh's to join their ranks, so I suppose I'll make the switch."

"Fitzhugh's is a good club," Gilmore said. "Sounds a good deal more interesting than the old one, at any rate."

"Indeed." Rhys laughed. "Should I try to get you an invitation, as well?"

Gilmore snorted. "That would be very kind. But I doubt you called me here to discuss clubs and social issues. We both knew this would likely happen."

"Sadly, yes. My social demise was sealed the moment my brother took his second wife." Rhys dropped his gaze to the floor beneath his feet. "And I suppose that is why I asked you here."

"Ah." Gilmore motioned him over to the chairs before the fire and retook the one he had abandoned upon Rhys's entry to the room. "Then it is about the lovely Pippa. I wondered when we'd talk about that subject."

"You knew we would?" Rhys asked, and his surprise was genuine.

Gilmore laughed. "From the first time I saw you with the woman, it was evident you were attracted to her and she to you."

"Well, Abigail encouraged me to discuss the issue with you."

Gilmore's eyebrows lifted. "The menace suggested this?"

Rhys narrowed his eyes. "Unless you'd rather discuss why the first Mrs. Montgomery knows your schedule well enough to tell me you were returning this morning and you shift in your seat every time she's mentioned."

"If she knows my schedule, it's likely because she's plotting some attack against my person," Gilmore huffed. "And I shift because she is the most frustrating person I have ever had the displeasure to know."

"Very well, a subject for another time, then," Rhys said. "She isn't wrong, though. I…need to talk to someone about Phillipa. And you are my dearest friend."

Gilmore was immediately serious. "Then tell me."

Rhys sighed and then gave a brief summary of his time in Bath with Phillipa. He offered few details, of course. He was no libertine, and this conversation was not to crow about a conquest.

"You are describing being in love with this woman," Gilmore said when he was finished. "This is not a mere affair."

Rhys pursed his lips. "I...am...in love with her. That isn't something I can deny."

"Though you should," Gilmore said, not unkindly.

Rhys flinched. "Perhaps, yes."

"You know it isn't just *perhaps*. A man who was banned from his club and shunned from social events should not link himself to the second wife of his bigamist brother. A man trying to rebuild his reputation *cannot* do that."

"I know all of that." Rhys ran a hand through his hair.

"But you don't want to do it," Gilmore said quietly as he sat back in his chair. "What do you want?"

Rhys shifted. If he said out loud what he wanted, he feared he'd never be able to fit it all back inside, to pretend he didn't desire it. To walk away from it. From her.

But Gilmore didn't budge. He just held his stare, waiting, daring him to be truthful, even for a moment. Rhys sighed. "I want to be with her. When I'm honest with myself, all I want is to be with her for the rest of my life."

"Knowing it will bash your recovery on the rocks?"

"Yes," Rhys said, and was surprised by the swiftness and certainty with which he spoke.

Gilmore draped his elbows over his knees. "Knowing it would make economic recovery all the harder?"

"Yes."

"Knowing it will tar her and that child with Erasmus's feather, with Society's brand, in a deeper way than they already are?"

Now Rhys hesitated and shook his head. "And there's the rub."

He got up and walked to the window, staring out at the street and seeing nothing. Gilmore let him for a moment and then he pushed to his own feet.

"She could be your mistress, you know. It's fashionable to be in love with those."

"Fuck." Rhys pivoted to face his friend. "I don't want to marry some woman I don't care about, just to maintain a position, and then keep the one I do love on the side as a secret. That would be cruel to everyone involved. I would be as bad as my brother."

Gilmore's face went hard. "No. You would not."

They stared at each other for a moment, and Rhys was oddly comforted. Gilmore was a difficult man to read, a harder man to know, but they had become close in the many years he had been lucky enough to call Gilmore friend. He knew the duke had his best interest at heart, even if he played devil's advocate to make Rhys explore every option. It was why Rhys had desired to speak to the man, after all.

Gilmore stepped closer. "It's complicated, trust that I know that. But answer me this, my friend: does your *happiness* play any part in your decision? Does hers?"

Rhys's lips parted. That was not a question he had expected Gilmore to ask. He'd thought the duke too pragmatic to consider such things.

But before he could respond, his butler stepped into the room. "I beg your pardon, my lord, Your Grace, but Mr. Gregory has arrived."

Rhys blinked and turned from Gilmore's seeing stare. "Thank you, Coleman. Please show him in, we are ready for him."

Gilmore hadn't turned from him, and when the butler left the room, he said, "Perhaps it should. Perhaps your mutual happiness should be the only consideration that truly matters."

"I just don't know," Rhys said, but nothing more as Owen Gregory entered the room.

"Good morning, gentlemen," he said, stretching a hand out first to Gilmore and then to Rhys.

"Good morning," Rhys said. "Thank you for coming at such an early hour."

"It's fine," Owen said. "My wife was calling on Phillipa and Abigail this morning. Told me not to expect her for lunch, which doesn't bode well for whatever trouble they may get up to."

"Led by Abigail?" Gilmore muttered. "We ought to call the guard."

Rhys ignored him and said, "I'm pleased to hear we may have you for the entire day. We may need you. Have you any updates regarding Rosie Stanton?"

Owen's expression grew serious. "Not much more than we had in the last few days. She has been seen at a few of her old haunts, but nothing concrete to help me determine why she is here and if she intends any nefarious deeds."

"Rosie Stanton?" Gilmore repeated. "I thought she left the country after Erasmus's unfortunate...accident."

The men caught the duke up on the turn of events that had occurred while he was out of town. "I feel increasingly uncomfortable with the woman's whereabouts being unknown," Rhys said when the background had been shared. "Especially since Phillipa and Kenley's new residence will be ready tomorrow, at least according to my solicitor. They'll move there and so will the guard I've put on them, but it's still a new environment and I'd prefer this be resolved before they go there."

"What do you suggest?" Owen asked.

"A sweep, rather like we did the first time we searched for her weeks ago. The three of us would make a formidable team," Rhys said. "Assuming you would be willing to assist, Gilmore."

The duke nodded. "Of course."

"Good." Rhys sighed in relief. "Why don't we start at the tavern where she worked for her father?"

"I agree," Owen said. "Though we didn't get much of a welcome the last time we went there, if you recall."

Rhys shrugged. "I don't care if they spit in my ale. I just want information."

"Very well," Owen said. "Shall we go now?"

They agreed to the idea, and Owen's rig was brought around since it was the only one without an identifying crest to draw attention. But as they all filed into the carriage, talking and scheming at once, Rhys felt no excitement at what he was doing. His conversation with Gilmore had stirred a great many questions in his mind.

Including whether or not his happiness was something he could ever consider again when planning his future.

Pippa followed Abigail from the carriage and stared at the house before her. The home Erasmus had shared with Rosie once they came to London. The place where she and her friends had been held captive, where Erasmus had died, weeks before. She shivered.

"I'm glad Celeste stayed back with Kenley. She was held at gunpoint here...I think it might have been upsetting."

"It's certainly upsetting to me," Abigail said.

"It's even more haunting all boarded up like this," Pippa murmured as she looked at the slabs of wood that crisscrossed the windows and the door. She could still see partially inside, and the house did look empty.

Abigail nodded. "Yes. Rhys said something about it before you left for Bath. He had it cleaned up, cleared out and closed. I assume he'll sell it once he gets a few more affairs in order."

Pippa turned her face. She was one of those affairs he had to get in order. Another weight on his shoulders. Perhaps being with her had temporarily lifted that weight, but it wasn't permanent. Perhaps nothing was, in the end.

She cleared her throat. "I still think we should knock."

Abigail signaled for her driver to remain where he was before they walked up together. She thrust her shoulders back and was the one to do the honors. But of course no one answered. The abandoned appearance of the house was true.

"Can I help you?"

Pippa jumped and the group turned. A woman had come down from one of the nearby homes, a broom in her hand, her hair in a kerchief.

"Er, yes," Pippa said. "Our old friend Rosie lived here once. We were trying to surprise her with a call."

The woman bent her head. "Oh, you won't find her here, I'm afraid. Poor lamb lost her husband a few weeks ago. Place was all closed up after."

"That is very sad," Pippa choked out.

"I don't suppose you know where she went then?" Abigail asked with a warm smile.

"Well, when I last saw her a few days ago, she said something about going back to where she started. Don't know what it meant, though."

Pippa stared. "Wait, you saw Rosie Stanton here…a few days ago?"

"Aye." The woman leaned on her broomstick. "The house was already boarded up, but she was coming from around the back. Had a satchel she was closing up and she said good afternoon and talked for a moment. Said she had to get a few last things that her husband left behind. I wished her good luck and off she went, walking back through town."

"Thank you," Abigail croaked.

The woman nodded, though she gave them all a strange look, indeed, before she went back to her own stoop and to her sweeping. Abigail motioned to the carriage before she spoke to her driver a moment. Then they both clambered in, taking their seats.

"I asked Thomas to hold a moment while we decide our next move," Abigail explained. "What do you make of it?"

Pippa shook her head. "She must have come back for something Erasmus hid here. Money or something else."

"It could have been anything," Abigail said with a frown. "Ill-gotten or properly so. But think of what she said. Back to the beginning."

"Her father's pub? The Stag and..." Pippa rocked her head back against the seat. "Oh, what was it called? Rhys said it a few times."

"The Stag and Serpent," Abigail finished with a purse of her lips. "In Cheapside."

"Do we dare go there?" Pippa asked.

"I was under the impression from talking to Owen and Celeste about it after you and Rhys left for Bath that it wasn't a terrible place," Abigail offered. "We might stand out a bit as two ladies, but I doubt we'd be in very great danger as long as we stay together."

"I say we try it." Pippa sighed. "God's teeth, this is like a never-ending nightmare."

"And this is how we end it." Abigail got out of the carriage and Pippa heard her say the pub name and the area of London.

They rolled out once she was settled back in place. It was nearly an hour's journey thanks to the traffic back in the city proper. Normally Pippa would have talked to Abigail, but they were both silent, the tension mounting with every passing mile.

"Is this a good idea?" Pippa whispered at last as they turned down a long street, one that would take them to their destination.

Abigail let out her breath in a shaky puff. "Probably not. But we're doing it for Kenley, aren't we? So we must go on."

Pippa reached out and caught Abigail's hand. They had been more uncomfortable with each other for a few weeks. It had hurt Pippa when she found out Abigail had more knowledge about Erasmus's bad deeds than she had once let on. But in that moment, all was forgiven.

"Thank you for everything you've done for me," she said. "For being one of my truest friends. It means everything and I will never forget it."

Abigail squeezed her fingers gently. "If we stand, we stand together. Always."

And then the carriage stopped and the future had to be faced. For better or for worse, and Pippa was happier than ever that she didn't do it alone.

CHAPTER 20

Rhys leaned his elbows on the bar top at the Stag and Serpent. It was only midday but the place was already busy with area men and women having their meal and a pint or two. He'd been here before, looking for the same woman they sought now. Only Owen had been there with him that time, and the reception they'd gotten was not friendly, to say the least.

But with the luncheon crowd buzzing, their threesome faded into the background much easier and no one seemed to care that they didn't truly belong here.

One of the serving maids stepped up near them, and Rhys flashed his brightest smile, adjusted his accent slightly and said, "We're looking for someone—do you think you could help?"

She edged a bit closer and let her gaze dance along all three of them. She smiled a bit flirtatiously. "Perhaps I could be convinced."

"Rosie Stanton. I believe she's the proprietor's daughter."

Her smile fell and turned to a glare. "I already told the women that I don't know where Rosie is. And if you ask too many questions around here, you might not like how it goes. Leave her be, she's been through enough." She flounced away.

Rhys blinked and stared at Owen and Gilmore. "The women?" he repeated, his heart sinking.

He turned to scan the crowd, this time looking for a face far more familiar than Rosie Stanton's. It was Owen who found them. He pointed across the tavern, his lips pursed. "There they are."

Rhys followed the indication, and as the crowd parted slightly, he saw Phillipa and Abigail sitting at a table in the corner. They were talking to a man whose back was to Rhys.

"Bloody hell," Gilmore grunted, and he sounded just as upset as Rhys felt.

Owen shook his head. "Makes me wonder where my wife is. Sentry duty? Walking the boards at a theatre somewhere? Robbing a coach for entertainment and profit?"

Rhys got up, his hands shaking with pure terror. Phillipa would come here, with only Abigail as protection? She would insert herself where she didn't belong without regard to her own well-being?

A thousand scenarios played out in his head all at once. Dangers and injuries and worse that could befall her for her foolhardy choice. And his stomach turned, his heart throbbed with each one.

"Come on." His voice wavered. "An explanation is in order, and I cannot wait to hear what it is."

Pippa's plan hadn't been going exactly as she had hoped. When they first arrived at the tavern, she and Abigail hadn't found anyone willing to talk to them. The man who had just left their table started out acting like he might be able to help, but it was soon clear he just wanted to flirt with the two of them.

Abigail sighed. "What a bloody waste of time."

Pippa looked off into the tavern, thinking about her answer, but before she could say anything, she caught a glimpse of Rhys through the crowd. Her mouth dropped open as she saw him weaving his way toward her. He wasn't alone, either. Owen Gregory and the Duke of Gilmore were at his side.

She caught Abigail's arm and shook it. "They're here!"

"Who is here?" Abigail asked. "Who is...oh!"

"Don't stand up," Rhys said through clenched teeth. He was almost vibrating with anger as he stared at her. "Do not make a scene."

"We're not making a scene," Abigail said, arching her brow at him. "The three of you are in more danger of doing that."

"She's right," Owen said. "It would behoove us to disperse quickly. Just tell me where my wife is and we can depart quickly and quietly."

Pippa forced herself to look away from Rhys, though she never stopped feeling his gaze on her. "Celeste didn't come," she said softly. "She's back at Abigail's house with Kenley. She didn't want to betray Owen by doing this behind his back."

"But *you* didn't mind doing so?" Rhys asked.

"Scolding can happen in the carriage," Owen said. "Come along."

Pippa and Abigail got up. Owen led the way, Gilmore marched behind Abigail as if he were a jailer, and Rhys took Pippa's arm to make up the rear.

"Rhys—" she began.

"Not a bloody word," he growled beneath his breath.

They exited into the street and immediately both their carriages arrived. Rhys motioned to Abigail's. "Owen, you and Gilmore take Abigail home."

He explained nothing else, but marched Pippa to what appeared to be Owen's rig. He waved her inside, his mouth tight, said something to the driver and then threw himself into the seat across from her and yanked the door shut hard.

"Rhys—" she tried again.

He shook his head. "*Not yet.*"

His gaze burned into her, unyielding even as he refused to talk to her. She shifted beneath it, desperate to do something to fix this, even though he had no right to such a strong reaction. She wasn't his, after all.

But every attempt she made to speak to him on the half-hour ride was thwarted with the same admonishment he'd already given. *Not yet.* And he continued to just stare at her, blue eyes narrow, emotions unreadable beyond upset.

Finally she flopped back against the seat, turned her face so she wouldn't have to confront that pointed stare, and looked out the window. At last they turned through a tall gate, onto a round drive in front of a massive home. She gasped as she realized this was *his* home. She had never been here, and she pressed a hand to the window as she observed the columned, towering building.

The carriage stopped and he got out, waving away the footman who came to assist her in doing the same. Rhys's hand flexed into the vehicle and she took it. But when her feet were on the ground, he didn't release her. He drew her up the stairs, past a gaping servant.

"My lord, may I—"

"Not now, Coleman," Rhys barked as he hauled Pippa down a long hallway and into a study. He released her and slammed the door behind them.

She paced away, taking in the room. Cherrywood-paneled walls, towering bookcases, beautiful artwork. This was a room that had likely been the haven for many a man who had shared Rhys's title over the years. And yet it still fit him. It was orderly and tidy, papers stacked just so, few knickknacks to disrupt the flow of the room.

Behind her, he rattled the bottles on the sideboard and poured himself a drink. He downed half of it and then slammed it down on the top. Amber liquid sloshed onto the wood, but he didn't seem to notice.

"What were you thinking?" he shouted, at last asking the question she had been waiting for since the moment he stalked up to the table at the Stag and Serpent.

"I was thinking that I need to establish what Rosie is doing," she snapped.

"You could have left that to us," he snapped.

"You think she would talk to you considering she murdered your brother in front of you? She is more likely to speak to me than to you. We were once...friendly, even if it was a lie. She *knows* me."

He stared at her, some of the heat fading from his expression. "That is...that is actually a good point."

"Thank you," she said softly.

"But it does not negate the fact that you went wandering into a place that could have been very dangerous—"

"I wasn't alone," she interrupted.

His gaze narrowed further as he continued, "—inquiring after a woman who committed murder, not to mention held you at gunpoint a mere few weeks ago."

"With Abigail at my side," she insisted again.

He fisted his hands. "I don't give a damn about Abigail." His tone was so sharp that it brought her up short. "How do you not fucking understand that, Phillipa? I'm upset *you* went there, I'm upset *you* endangered yourself."

Here they were, right back to where they'd started. Loving each other without any hope that it could go beyond a moment in time. She drew a few breaths to calm herself, since he didn't seem to be able to do so.

"What Rosie did before, she did thanks to Erasmus's lies and prodding. I felt certain she wasn't a danger to me again, so I had to take the risk for Kenley."

She thought that would appease him, make him see the value in what she'd done. Instead, he took a long step toward her, closing the gap between them. "How many ways can I say it, Phillipa? I don't want you taking risks at all. Not for anyone, even Kenley. You are too...precious to me."

She bent her head as pain slashed through her, powerful and hot. "Rhys," she whispered.

He didn't answer, but put a hand beneath her chin, tilting her face toward his. She forced herself to look at him, drank him in, his beautiful face so close to hers, his bright eyes dilated with desire and emotion. And when he took her lips, she didn't pull away. She couldn't. She wanted this too much for prudence.

And once he touched her? Well, there was no such thing as prudence anymore. His fingers dug into her hair, tilting her face for more access to her mouth. She tugged the buttons of his coat, popping one off before she drew her hands inside, reveling in his warmth as she bunched her fingers against his muscular back.

He pushed her across the room until her backside bumped his desk, and then he lifted her there. His hands were shaking as he unfastened her dress, but hers were too while she shoved his jacket aside and went to work on his shirt. His mouth dragged down her throat, his teeth scraping delicate skin, his fingers pushing into her hips as he tugged her closer.

She whispered his name against his shoulder while she pulled his shirt from his trousers. He released her long enough to pull it over his head and she murmured her approval before she latched her mouth against his chest. She swirled her tongue around one flat nipple and traced her hand down his stomach.

He pulled away from her, panting, and for a moment she thought he might end this madness. Instead he tugged her from the desk, yanked her dress down and kicked it aside. Now he placed her back on the desk and stepped between her legs, her chemise pushed up, her drawers parted, and it wouldn't take anything for him claim her.

Only he didn't. His mouth slowed on hers, like he was savoring her now. She wrapped her arms around him more tightly, surrendering to his heat and his strength, drawing in his scent and memorizing all of it. One of his hands slid down her side and wedged between their bodies. He dipped past the gap in her drawers and his fingers found her sex.

She dropped her head back with a gasp of pleasure as he traced her entrance. He sucked her throat as he dipped one finger inside to where she was already wet and aching. She gripped him, grinding against even this small invasion, harder when he added a second finger.

He continued to kiss her throat as he began to pump into her, firmer and faster, curling his fingers against some hidden place deep within her. Her hips moved out of her own control to find the pleasure he was trying to draw from her. It was right there, right on the edge, some new place she had never found but desperately wanted to conquer.

The orgasm hit her and she bowed her back against his free arm. Items on his desk fell, thanks to how they were rocking it, but none of it mattered. Nothing mattered except for the electric pleasure roaring through her veins as he pleasured her.

The ripples of release hadn't even fully faded when she managed to tug open the buttons on his fly front. She gripped his cock as the fabric fell away, pulling him closer by the hard evidence of his desire for her.

"I want this," she murmured as she tilted her head to kiss him again.

He didn't deny her. He slid her forward almost all the way to the edge of the desk and aligned their bodies. Then he was driving home through her still rippling sex. He cupped her backside and ground against her, bringing her back up the side of the mountain she had just fallen down. He pounded into her, mercilessly, like he was punishing her for endangering herself. Only the punishment was pure pleasure. She gripped his bare shoulders, her nails abrading his skin as she worked her body against his. It was a war and yet they both wanted the same thing.

When she came again, it was harder than before, the pleasure more focused, and she couldn't help but cry out in the quiet room. He caught her screams with his mouth, but gave her no quarter as she came and came. Only when she went weak in his arms did he thrust a few more times, pull out and explode between them with a guttural cry.

For what felt like a lifetime, they remained that way. Their arms around each other, their sweat mingling. She didn't want to let him go, she didn't want to return to the reality that was so cold when what they shared could warm her forever. Except it couldn't.

He pressed a kiss into the spot where her shoulder and her neck met. "Did you and Abigail find anything out?"

She laughed because she couldn't help but do so. "Oh, *now* you want to benefit from the actions you berated me for a few moments ago."

"I don't think I was *berating* you a few moments ago," he said as he lifted his gaze to spear hers. "Or would you argue?"

She smiled. "Never with you. Not about that."

He kissed her and she sighed against his lips. "We didn't find out anything directly," she admitted. "Though I wouldn't call what we did a lost cause."

"No?" he asked.

She shrugged. "Word will filter back to her that we're looking. She might reach out to me."

His mouth twitched. "Again, very dangerous. I don't like it."

"I know you don't. But that doesn't mean it's the wrong move."

"Will you at least promise to tell me or Owen if she does reach out to you?"

She traced his face with her fingers. "I will. Though I'm certain you will be very busy now that you're back in London."

"Not as busy as you think." He straightened up and tucked himself back into his trousers. She could see the lines of trouble on his face as he refastened them.

"Why?" she asked.

He leaned on the desk beside her, his hands right next to hers on the edge. She rested her head on his shoulder. For a moment it was quiet, but she could sense the trouble in him.

"I-I shouldn't say more," he said.

She lifted her head and stared at him. "Why?" He met her gaze and her lips parted. "Something happened?"

"I shouldn't trouble you with it," he said. "It's my problem. I've just grown accustomed to...to talking to you."

"But you don't want to talk to me about this," she whispered. "What happened, Rhys?"

He shook his head. "I was banned from my club."

Her eyes immediately filled with tears. "Because of Erasmus. Because of all of us."

"Not because of you," he said, but they both knew it was a lie. "Not your fault, at any rate."

Perhaps it wasn't. Not directly. She had unwisely married a man who had convinced her that he might make her life more interesting. She had told herself she loved him and wanted the life he pretended to create. That made her foolish, but not culpable for all that had happened next.

But the truth still remained that people would invoke her name when they maligned Rhys. And that would fade with time if she faded back, too. But by being with him, loving him? That could only destroy him all the more.

Her actions were her own fault, her own responsibility.

She pushed off the desk and grabbed for her gown. He watched her as she stepped into it and refastened herself. "Phillipa," he said softly.

She refused to look at him as she smoothed her curls as best she could. "Please don't."

"Please don't what?" he asked as he got up from the desk and caught her arm, pulling her closer.

She pressed both hands to the solid warmth of his chest and moved away again. "Please don't make this harder than it is."

"Make what harder?"

In that moment she hated him for making her say the worst word in the world. Hated everything that had brought them here. "Goodbye."

~

P hillipa's voice trembled as she said that word, and yet it had as much power as a curse shouted from the heavens themselves.

"After what just happened, you can't mean that," he said. "There must be some other way."

"There isn't. There never has been. And I've danced around this, but too much has happened for me to keep doing that."

"Nothing has happened," he said, and wished he could take back admitting he'd lost his club membership. "Society does this. It shuns and it accepts. There is a path back and I'm walking it. I've already been invited to another club, it will just be different. It has nothing to do with you."

"It has *everything* to do with me. And if I keep coming back to you, keep giving in to this thing we probably never should have begun, I will destroy you forever. There will be no path." She cupped his cheeks. "I can't do that."

"What if I'm willing to accept those consequences?" he asked.

Her face crumpled, as if he'd said something horrible instead of wonderful. "And what, Rhys? Keep me as a mistress? Make me..." She trailed off as if she couldn't even say any other alternative. "No. It would destroy you. And I...I care too much for you to do that. We have to let go."

"No," he said, reaching for her.

She dodged. "Yes."

"No!" he repeated, and this time he did catch her. He drew her to him, he kissed her. For a moment she was soft in his arms, but then she pushed away again.

"Yes," she whispered. "The boundaries we tried to put up...they aren't enough, that's clear. I cannot see you at all. I'll make sure Kenley is brought to you regularly for visits. Nan will accompany him. I'll send messages to you to keep you apprised about his health or well-being through our friends or a solicitor. And if that is too hard, perhaps it would be best for you and for him if I..." Her breath caught. "If I left."

He staggered back. "Left him. Left me?"

She nodded. "He's young and surrounded by people who will love and protect him. It would break my heart to lose him, but this would be a better time to do it than in a year or five years. A last resort if I can't do what I need to do."

"Which is to leave me." He heard the flatness to his tone. Inside he felt anything but flat, though. He felt like someone was tearing him to pieces.

She sobbed out a breath and stepped back toward him. She caught his cheeks, and her eyes met his. He saw her struggle, saw her love for him even though she had never said it. Saw all her regrets and fear and heartbreak, the very same things that were mirrored in his own heart.

"If I could do anything else, I would do it," she choked out.

She brushed her mouth to his, then pressed her forehead against his for a moment. And at last she pulled back. She turned to leave and he knew he would let her. Because she wasn't wrong in all of her assessments of what would happen if he made her stay.

But as she reached the door, he stepped toward her. "I have to know one thing."

She kept her back to him, her shoulders slumped forward. "What is it?"

"If I'd been to your father's assembly room in Bath before you met my brother. If I had found you there first, if you and I had met—"

She pivoted to face him, her cheeks pale and her eyes brimming with tears. "That is a cruel question."

"And I want the answer," he pressed.

She fisted her hands at her sides, fingers flexing open and closed. "If I had met you first, there never would have been anyone but you, Rhys. It would have always been you."

She said nothing more, but pivoted on her heel and ran from the room, leaving him alone. Leaving him broken. Leaving him lost.

CHAPTER 21

I t had been a week since her last encounter with Rhys, and Pippa still woke up thinking about him every morning. When she slept, that was. Abigail and Celeste had mentioned how tired she looked, Pippa saw it in the mirror herself. The circles beneath her eyes were dark and deep. But when her friends pressed, she always blamed the exhaustion on all the excitement that had been happening in the past seven days.

And she supposed that's what they believed, even if they exchanged worried glances when they thought she wasn't looking. After all, the home Rhys had selected for Kenley had been readied at last. She had moved the boy there three days before and they were settling in.

Rhys, of course, had not made an appearance there. He was honoring her request that he back away, that he sever whatever they had shared. Nan had even taken Kenley to see him on the moving day so the child wouldn't be underfoot.

Life was becoming what it should be. Pippa liked the part of London where they lived. It was a solid middle-class neighborhood near a park and shops. She wasn't far from Abigail or Celeste, so she could visit often.

She'd even received an invitation to join Lady Lena's, a salon operated by one of Celeste's good friends. It was a coveted invitation and she looked forward to attending, though she wasn't sure of the reception she might receive.

It all should have amounted to peace for her, this plan set in motion at last. But she felt nothing like it.

"God, don't get maudlin now," she scolded herself as she got up from the settee where she had been trying to read and set her book aside.

It was dark outside, and she went to the window to look at the lamplight in the street. Carriages bustled by and she strained to see the crests on the doors. Perhaps one of them was Rhys's.

"Mrs. Montgomery?"

Pippa turned with a smile for Mrs. Barton. "You know, I think the time has come to change what you call me. I was never married, was I? Not in truth. I don't want to carry Erasmus's name anymore. It is more fitting to call me Miss Windridge. Or even Pippa, as I'm no longer your mistress."

Mrs. Barton shifted as if that made her uncomfortable. "I understand. Thought I cannot agree that you are not the mistress of this house."

"I'm not, though. In truth, we all are in service of Kenley now, me included. I'm no less of a servant than you or Mr. Barton."

Mrs. Barton wrinkled her brow. "That will take some getting used to, ma'am...miss?"

Pippa laughed despite her down mood. "We will figure it out together, won't we? What can I do aside from make you very uncomfortable, as I have accidentally done?"

"Not at all, Miss Windridge." Mrs. Barton glanced over her shoulder. "Nan got Kenley down about half an hour ago. Are we still expecting Lord Leighton's solicitor tomorrow afternoon?"

Pippa nodded. "Yes. The letter I received today from the man said two o'clock. I think he's going to discuss the allowance for the household, as well as what we can expect for Kenley's future funds."

"Will we be seeing Lord Leighton, as well?"

Pippa opened her mouth but could not make a sound as she tried to push aside the feelings that question stirred in her. "No. I do not think Lord Leighton will often call here, if ever. He must focus on the great deal of work he has to do, and we must focus on Kenley."

Mrs. Barton's gaze flashed with something remarkably like pity for a moment, but she wiped it away and both she and Pippa pretended it had not been there. "Very good."

Pippa forced another smile. "Is that all?"

"Yes, miss." Mrs. Barton nodded and then slipped from the room.

When she was gone, Pippa sighed. Despite whatever she said to Mrs. Barton, she had no idea what she was, who she was, anymore. She wanted so desperately just to run away. To escape the sorrow that went along with her acceptance of her position in Society. Her acceptance that Rhys would not be hers.

Except she couldn't run. Because of Kenley. And in that moment, she longed to see him. He would center her, remind her what was worth all the pain, all the loss she was enduring now.

She climbed the stairs and turned down toward his nursery. She gently opened the door and stepped inside. To her surprise, the room wasn't dark as it should have been this time of night, but lit with candles. Kenley wasn't in his cradle.

No, he was being held by Rosie Stanton.

Her dark hair was a little wild and her gaze teary as she snapped it from the baby in her arms to Pippa as she stepped into the room. Neither of them breathed for what felt like a lifetime.

Pippa's heart throbbed as she whispered, "Rosie, please put him down."

But Rosie did not release the half-asleep child. She just shook her head and said, "Stay where you are now. Don't make me do something we'll both regret."

～

R hys stared into the dancing flames of the fire in his parlor, his mind spinning away with their mesmerizing swirl. It took him to one place, one person, the one he had to forget. The one he couldn't forget. Phillipa might have been right that they couldn't pretend there was a future, but damn, it was hard to accept.

He had been struggling with it for a week. How many times had he ridden past her new home and stared up in the hopes of seeing her at the window? How many times had he asked his solicitor about Kenley because he wanted the man to say *Phillipa Montgomery* and remind Rhys that she wasn't some fantasy he'd conjured in his head?

He felt like he was going mad.

"And so I decided to walk with the monkey and ride the clown."

He blinked at the discordant words that Owen Gregory was saying and pivoted to face the investigator with a shake of his head. "What was that?"

"Ah, I wondered how long it would take for you to notice that I was speaking gibberish," Owen said with a laugh. "Seven full minutes of me dancing with milk maids and deciding to crown myself King of Spain."

"Seven?" Rhys repeated as his cheeks heated with embarrassment.

Owen shrugged. "If the clock on the mantel you're gripping is correct. You were also so distracted that you even agreed to up my hourly rate to one thousand pounds. Shall I open a line of credit for you, my lord, and tell Celeste to start buying herself magnificent jewels?"

Rhys shook his head with a smile at the teasing. "Obviously I was woolgathering. I apologize, that does not make me a good host in the slightest."

"I can handle a poor host. You are certainly not one of those normally. My larger concern is that you have not been yourself for days."

"I am…preoccupied with discovering the whereabouts of Rosie Stanton," Rhys said. "And I'm certain you answered this question while I was miles away, but bear with me and do it again. Where are we in the search for her?"

"All of us descending on her father's tavern did not do us any good," Owen admitted. "Any and all acquaintances are silent as the grave. There is still no indication Rosie has departed the country, but she has gone deep underground. I've lost her trail and I fear I failed you."

Rhys's stomach turned. "Not your fault. I'm sure my brother taught her all his tricks for subterfuge when they were making their plans." He gripped his hands at his sides as rage boiled in him. "The woman pretended to be Phillipa's friend and servant, all the while carrying on with my brother under her nose."

Owen pursed his lips. "Then I suppose one could assume she has skills in chicanery."

"And every reason to hide from me," Rhys said. "The official declaration of Erasmus's death might read as suicide now, but we all know that Rosie struck my brother down all those weeks ago. She must fear reprisal from me."

"You have no interest in such a thing, though?" Owen asked. "You never talk about doing anything to claim revenge."

"I don't want it." Rhys ran a hand through his hair. "My brother and I weren't close and it was a complicated situation. Even Rosie was a victim, no matter if she helped Erasmus along the way. I certainly don't want to stir it back up again. I just want to know where she is so that I can keep Kenley and Phillipa safe."

"I'll keep searching," Owen promised. "And keep both you and Pippa apprised of the situation. Though I must say, it would be easier if I could make these reports to you together rather than separately."

Rhys caught his breath. He would love that, too, just to see Phillipa. Just to breathe the air near her and scent the citrus fragrance of her hair and skin. And there he went again, off on trails of thought that could only bring him heartache.

"Not possible," he said softly.

Owen leaned back in his chair and folded his arms. His bright eyes held Rhys's and he shook his head. "Do you think I'm bad at what I do?"

Rhys drew back at the question. "I would be a fool to keep you on my payroll if I did. Certainly I'd be a fool to up your rate to a thousand pounds an hour." Owen laughed at that quip and Rhys continued, "What makes you ask me such a silly thing? Fishing for compliments doesn't seem your manner."

"It isn't, though I do enjoy a compliment now and then."

Rhys chuckled. "I'll endeavor to give more then, to satisfy you."

"I'd appreciate it. But I'm asking you the question because you clearly think I'm blind," Owen said, "to not see that your mood is because of Pippa and hers is because of you."

"Pippa is in a mood?" Rhys asked, and wished he sounded more nonchalant about the answer.

"Yes. She's distracted and moping in almost equal measure to you." Owen speared him with a knowing glance. "You two are quite the pair. So why don't you stop staring into the fire like you're going to find what you've lost in the flames, sit down and have a conversation with me?"

Rhys arched a brow as he reached for his most lord-of-the-manor tone. "How dare you?"

Owen looked less than impressed. "A moment ago I was your employee and you could put me in line with that arched brow, my lord. But right now I'm your friend. And I *know* I'm your friend because you've told me that I am. Your *friend* isn't going to fall all over himself just because you're the sixteenth Earl of Leighton or whatever is so very fancy about your title."

Rhys stared at Owen and then he sat down as he had been asked. "The tenth earl," he corrected under his breath.

"Begging your pardon." Owen tilted his head in a facsimile of a bow. "Please, *talk* to me. Everyone in your life can see you and Pippa are both suffering and all anyone wants to do is help. Let me be of assistance here and now."

Rhys rubbed his hands against his thighs. "I almost don't see a point in talking. Not just to you, but to anyone. While I appreciate the concern from you, Celeste, Abigail and Gilmore, there is nothing *any* of you can do. What I want is impossible. Phillipa has said as much. Worse is that even though I hate it, I know she's not wrong."

Owen lifted his brows. "And why exactly can't you have what you want?"

"Because of scandal, because of ruin, because of everything there is to lose, because of Erasmus Fucking Montgomery and the fact that he's my brother and her...almost husband." Rhys threw his hands up in frustration. "Bloody fucking hell."

Swearing should have helped. It didn't.

Owen arched his brow at the uncharacteristic outburst. "Is that all or do you need a few more curses? I can be creative if you need suggestions."

"No, that will do for now," Rhys said. "But you must see that there is no point in the discussion, which is why, friend or not, I haven't entertained the topic with you or Gilmore or anyone else."

Owen's expression was inscrutable. Very much the face of him as an investigator, the same face Rhys had stared into many times when Owen was looking into his brother's murder.

"Tell me something, Lord Leighton," Owen said, and now his tone was that of an investigator, as well. "This scandal, it exists no matter what, doesn't it?"

Rhys snorted out a humorless laugh. "Oh, it does. I am reminded any time I go into public or encounter a person I thought was a friend who now shuns me."

"And it will last for some time," Owen pressed. "Months. Years, even."

Rhys glared at him. "Yes, thank you so much for pointing that out. I'm very glad we talked, I feel so much better."

Owen chuckled at the dry tone. "I admit that didn't sound right. It wasn't an attempt to rub your nose in the facts. I only meant that this *is* happening. And because of the way Society works, there isn't much that can change it."

"I suppose not. It must play out however it does, for however long those in charge decide to deny me," Rhys said. "Not that the clarification was much better, *Mr. Gregory.*"

"Bear with me," Owen said, raising his hands in what seemed like surrender. "I'm doing an exceedingly poor job making what I think is a good point. Answer me this: do you want to spend the next months, years, perhaps even the rest of your life, carrying this scandal on your back alone? Or would you like to do alongside a partner? A friend? The love of your life?"

Rhys stared at him. Suddenly it was like he had been punched in the chest or dragged under the water. The room seemed to fade. Owen sounded far away, and everything began to spin.

"You are miserable, correct?" Owen asked through the fog.

"Yes," Rhys choked out.

"I can attest that I would rather be miserable and have Celeste by my side than be what I used to call happy without her." Owen smiled slightly. "She makes it better."

"What? What does she make better?"

Rhys knew the answer. He knew it even before Owen said, "*Everything.*"

Rhys shook his head. "Phillipa...she would never relent, even if I did."

"Because she can't take the trouble?" Owen asked.

Rhys fought a sudden desire to punch Owen in the nose. He thought that was the desired effect, in truth. Owen wanted him to defend Phillipa. "Of course not. She wants to...to protect me."

"Even better. You clearly wish to protect her, as well. But it's all the more powerful if you choose to protect each other."

Rhys got to his feet and shook his head. "You make it sound so easy."

"It *is* easy!" Owen insisted.

"Because you and Celeste didn't have as many barriers to your happiness."

Owen shrugged. "Different barriers, not no barriers. But perhaps that isn't your true hesitation. Perhaps you don't want to be with her as much as the rest of us have guessed."

Rhys glared at him. "Of course I do. I have been in love with her for weeks and weeks. Thoughts of her torment me all day, haunt me all night. I can taste her on my tongue even though it's been days since I kissed her. I can hear her in my ear with such clarity that I sometimes turn and hope she'll be there. She is the only person I wish to talk to about all these difficulties I am facing. The only person I want to talk to about the joys, as well. The only person I want to see every day of my life until the last."

Owen drew back a fraction at the intensity of the confession. Rhys could hardly blame him, but once he started, it had been virtually impossible to stop.

"And yet..." Owen got up and cocked his head, almost in question. "...you stand here in your parlor with me."

Rhys huffed out a breath. "What would you have me do? Go to her house and refuse to leave until Phillipa hears me declare my love for her? Until she agrees to be mine, no matter the obstacles we have yet to face?"

He heard the words and stopped, staring at Owen as the true reality of the situation hit him in the chest. Took his air. Made his hands begin to shake. "That is...that's exactly what I have to do, isn't it? I have to do that now."

Owen smiled. "I would *highly* recommend it."

Terror struck Rhys at the thought, but it was a beautiful fear. The fear of perhaps getting what one wanted, of losing it, of taking a gamble that could bring either outcome. Yes, it would be difficult. And she might say no at first, determined to save him from himself.

But that didn't mean he shouldn't risk it. He smoothed his jacket and looked down at himself, then turned to glance around the room. "I need a horse," he muttered.

"Come then," Owen said, laughing at Rhys's confusion. He caught Rhys's elbow and dragged him from the room. "Coleman," he called out.

The butler appeared momentarily. "Yes, Mr. Gregory?"

"The earl needs his horse. And I suppose I also need mine, since I will be going home to tell my wife that something wonderful may happen tonight."

Coleman bowed out the door to call for the footmen to fetch the animals. As he did so, Rhys turned to Owen. "I almost fear the idea that it could be wonderful."

"You shouldn't," Owen assured him. "God knows the woman is head over heels in love with you, as well. I have every confidence that you are going to arrive at her home tonight to find good things, a welcome you deserve, and a happiness that I know will last you a lifetime."

The horses were brought 'round and Owen motioned to Rhys's. Rhys swung up and glanced down at his friend. "I do hope you are correct, my friend. Thank you for the encouragement."

"I only made you see what you already knew," Owen said, then patted the horse's flank. "Off with you."

Rhys urged the horse into a trot out the gate and then faster down the street. Now that he knew what he wanted for the rest of his life, he wanted that moment to begin as soon as possible. And he could only hope that Owen was right. That he would find a warm welcome and a very happy ending to this tale tonight.

CHAPTER 22

Pippa's hands shook as she reached behind her and shut the door quietly. She had no idea what Rosie Stanton's plans were, but the threat of her words were clear. Certainly Pippa didn't want to involve the Bartons or Nan in whatever would happen next.

"Rosie," she said as calmly and gently as she could, in the hopes her composure would keep the other woman at ease. "Please. Think this through, whatever you plan to do."

She moved a step forward, and Rosie shook her head. "I have a gun," she said softly. "I don't want to pull it out while I'm holding Kenley, but if you give me no choice, then I will."

Pippa froze immediately, for her own good, but also for his. Kenley, meanwhile, had lifted his tired head from Rosie's shoulder and now looked at Pippa. He smiled a little, then glanced at his mother nervously before he reached for Pippa.

Rosie tried to turn him so he wouldn't see her, but Kenley continued to grasp for Pippa with increasingly anxious grunts and cries.

"He wants you," Rosie spat at last. "I am his mother and he reaches for you."

Pippa shook her head. "It is only because I have spent so much time with him. It has been months since he's seen you, so you are a stranger to him. But if he saw you more, he would be comfortable."

Rosie blinked, as if she hadn't fathomed that abandoning her child for months on end might have an effect on the quality of their relationship. She stared at the boy. "He is so much bigger," she breathed, almost to herself.

Pippa nodded. "He is. He's doing very well. Growing every day. He's beginning to make noises that are somewhat like words, and he can point to what he wants. He shifts himself around on the ground without help and he's begun eyeing things to pull himself up with. He's a good boy, Rosie. You should be exceptionally proud of him."

Rosie's eyes filled with tears that she blinked away. Her mouth hardened. "And you're playing mother to him, even though you're barren as a grave."

Pippa flinched. There had been times, especially when Rosie was pregnant, long before she knew the awful truth of the father of her maid's child, that she had been jealous of her impending mother-hood. But God's teeth, she was glad Erasmus Montgomery hadn't gotten her with child. It would have made everything so much worse.

"I don't have any illusions that I am his mother," she said. "Though I do love him. I could not love him more if he was my own."

Rosie's expression softened, and Pippa might have said more on the subject to appease her. But before she could, the door to the nursery opened. She pivoted and, to her shock, Rhys stepped inside, a broad smile on his handsome face.

"Phillipa, there you are, you—" He broke off as his gaze moved past her to Rosie. His smile fell, and he caught Pippa's arm and dragged her behind him. As he did so, she realized that Rosie had, indeed, pulled the gun she had claimed to have a few moments before.

It seemed Kenley could feel the fearful shift in the room as much as any of them because he began to wail. Softly at first, but with growing intensity. Rosie flashed her gaze on him, a combination of worry and annoyance.

"What are you doing here?" Rhys's voice was thick with fear and an undercurrent of anger. Rosie's hand began to shake in reaction, and Pippa's stomach turned. If she didn't calm the situation again, they might all be dead soon.

She drew in a deep breath and pushed back in front of him. He caught her arm once more, his eyes going wide that she would put herself in the potential line of fire. She met his gaze and gently shook her head, pleading silently for him to trust her. They stared at each other for a fraction of a moment, but she saw him soften, saw his faith in her override his drive to protect her. He released her arm, though he didn't look happy about it, and allowed her to make herself the target first.

"Rosie and I are just talking, Lord Leighton. We are *talking*, do you understand?" She returned her attention to Rosie. "Put the gun away, my dear. No one is threatening you, I promise."

"Of course he is," Rosie whispered, flicking the gun barrel over Pippa's shoulder in Rhys's direction, an action that made Pippa's stomach turn with every movement. At this range, the woman could kill them both with one shot. "We all know that I killed Erasmus." Her voice broke. "I killed him."

"You loved him," Pippa whispered. "Everyone knows that, too. Rhys knows that. Don't you?"

Rhys's fingers gently wrapped around Pippa's upper arms, and for a moment she leaned back against his chest. She didn't want him here, endangered by Rosie's terror. His presence enflaming that fear all the more. And yet she was so comforted by him. At least she wasn't alone.

"I know you loved him," Rhys said. "I know that you didn't want to hurt him. That you were driven to harm him by what he said and did, that he had a bigger hand in all of this than anyone else. I don't want revenge on you, I swear that to you now."

"And what about the guard? The government. Don't they want me transported or hanged for killing the second son of an earl?" Rosie spat. "Can't let a little person do something like that, can you?"

Rhys shook his head. "Any interested authorities have been told that my brother's death was accidental. No one knows Erasmus was shot or that you shot him. Going back on that would only make the situation he created worse..." He cocked his head, as if he were reading the woman threatening them. "Worse for me."

Rosie shifted. "He left you a mess, didn't he?"

"He did. And I'm trying to clean it up as best I can for myself. And for everyone he harmed. *Everyone*, Rosie."

Rosie looked uncertain, though she lowered the gun a little as Kenley continued to cry in her arms. "You were looking for me. If not to trap, to take, then why?"

"To understand you," Pippa said softly. "To try to figure out why you had been seen trying to obtain passage west but never took it...twice."

Rosie was quiet a moment. "I-I wanted to leave," she whispered. "I knew I had to run after what I did. But I kept thinking of Kenley. Erasmus wanted to abandon him, and that's why I shot him. What kind of mother would I be if I did the same thing? So I stayed, even though I knew it was foolhardy."

"You want to protect your son," Rhys said. "Just as we do."

Rosie's eyes narrowed. "You *hated* your brother. Why would you want to protect his bastard child?"

Pippa reached up to cover Rhys's hand, which tightened on her arm. She felt the strain in him, the pain amidst the fear. "I had problems with my brother," he admitted at last. "But I don't hate his son. The truth is that I...I love him, just as Phillipa does."

He released Phillipa and took a step past her, toward Rosie. She lifted the gun again and Pippa gasped, but Rhys didn't let her pass. "I would do anything to protect that child, Rosie. Anything to protect

Phillipa. Even if it means walking into the barrel of your gun to comfort him as he's weeping."

He reached out his arms toward Kenley, and Pippa covered her mouth with both hands. She was certain Rosie would pull the trigger. That she would be forced to watch Rhys bleed out on the floor as she had watched Erasmus do weeks before.

Only she didn't. Instead, Rosie released Kenley as Rhys took him. He pivoted swiftly and handed him over to Pippa. She clutched his warm, solid weight and backed away, out of the line of the gun's sights. Kenley calmed as she held him, burying his head into her shoulder with a whimper of what sounded like exhausted relief.

Rhys turned back to Rosie. She still trained her gun on him, but her wrist had gone slack. Her eyes were filled with tears. She looked...lost. And despite all she had done, despite what she'd put Pippa through tonight and many other nights, Pippa felt sorry for her.

"You loved my brother for a long time, and you were denied happiness because of my father," Rhys said. "I cannot imagine what you endured."

He reached out and wrapped his hand around the barrel of the pistol. He pushed it so it no longer pointed at his chest and then twisted so that Rosie was forced to release it. Once she had, she collapsed to her knees on the floor, sobbing.

Rhys pocketed the gun, yet made no move to take this woman into custody of any kind. Pippa moved toward him, took his hand as they stared down at the woman at their feet.

"What will you do for my child?" Rosie sobbed.

"I will provide the same life for him that I would give my own son," Rhys promised. "I will protect him, guide him, love him. He will want for nothing that I can provide."

Rosie's tears subsided a bit with that promise, and she looked up at him, at Pippa. "You will give him a family?" she whispered. "A future? The two of you?"

Pippa blinked because she realized that Rosie assumed she and

Rhys would be together. Not a fact that was likely to come to pass, but it didn't matter. What mattered was keeping Kenley secure.

"Yes," she said.

"I don't want to be here anymore," Rosie whimpered. "In London, I mean, in England. I miss Erasmus, I *hate* what I did to him. Everything here haunts me. I thought I could come here and take Kenley and make a life. But when I saw him...he haunted me too. He has so much of Erasmus in him."

"He does," Pippa agreed. "But also so much of you. He is yours, I don't want you to think I don't know it."

Rosie sobbed a little harder. "I want to start a new life, but the idea of leaving him behind, even if I know he could be happy with you..."

Pippa handed Kenley off to Rhys and sank to her knees in front of the other woman. She took her hands gently. "I will write to you wherever you end up. I will give you all the news of him. And when he is older, old enough to understand, perhaps you can one day meet with him again."

She meant those words as she said them. Imperfect or not, troubled or not, this woman was Kenley's mother. They had a right to know each other, to love each other. She couldn't deny the boy that any more than she would deny him any other part of his history.

"You would do that?" Rosie hiccupped.

"She would," Rhys said. "She is too good not to keep a promise. And I will make one too. I will provide you the funds for your trip, and a little to start anew, wherever you go. I owe you that. My brother owed you more."

Rosie was still for a moment, staring up at the baby once more. Then she slowly got to her feet and Pippa followed her. Rosie sucked in a shaky breath and then nodded. "Taking care of him on my own wouldn't be easy...for either of us. And I don't know if I could ever look at him and not see what I...what I did." She let out a hiccupping sob before she continued, "It's obvious he loves you both. So if you love him in return, then this would be the best place for him." There was relief on her face alongside the deep sadness. "I can start over and he can too."

Rhys glanced at Pippa and she saw what he wanted to do. She nodded slowly, though it was frightening to do so. Right, but terrifying. He drew in a long breath and then offered Kenley back to his mother.

"Say goodbye?" he said softly.

Rosie's expression collapsed, and she nodded as tears began to stream down her face. She held out her arms, and this time Kenley glanced at Rhys and Pippa. Since both of them were smiling, trying to be as ease with this as possible, he seemed to accept it better. He allowed himself to be taken, though he kept looking back at Pippa over his mother's shoulder.

Rosie paced away from them, to the corner of the room. She spoke softly to her son, words that weren't for Pippa and Rhys. Pippa turned into Rhys's side as they watched the heartbreaking scene, the hopeful scene. An ending, yes, but a beginning all at once. This woman Pippa had once hated, then feared, she found herself admiring and loving because she had decided to do what was best for her child.

After a little time passed, Rosie came back. She handed Kenley over to Pippa, then wiped her eyes with the back of her hand. "I'm at Garrison House on the west end of Whitechapel. I'll wait there for whoever you send to arrange the particulars."

"You're putting your faith in me, in us," Rhys said. "And I will not let you down."

Rosie shrugged and the harder exterior returned. She glanced at Kenley one last time and then moved to the window. "I'll go the way I came." Her voice wavered. "Goodbye."

She disappeared, and Pippa gasped in a breath and hugged Kenley tight as Rhys rushed over to close and lock the window securely. When he turned back, his face was drawn and pale. He said nothing as he crossed the room and embraced Pippa and Kenley, the three of them clinging to each other for what felt like a lifetime, but still not enough. And it would never be enough.

Perhaps what she wanted wasn't something she could have, but Pippa still held tightly to this man she loved and celebrated the fact that Kenley was safe, they were both uninjured, and the future was looking brighter, at least for the boy squirming in her arms between them.

CHAPTER 23

P hillipa's hands hadn't stopped shaking since Rosie made her great escape. They still did so as she tucked the blanket around Kenley's little form. For a moment, she and Rhys stood together over him, watching as he drifted back into the sleep his grieving mother had interrupted.

Rhys wrapped an arm around Phillipa's waist, and she rested her head against his shoulder. This was how he wanted life to be forever. Well, minus the threats, the terror of coming into the nursery to find her at the whims of a woman who had already killed once.

He shivered just to recall it.

"She loves him," Phillipa said softly.

He glanced down at her. Despite everything his brother had done to this woman, everything her parents had done, everything Rosie Stanton had done...she had not become bitter or cold or hard. She was still warm and wonderful, willing to see the best in others, in him. Dear God, but he loved her.

"She does," he said. "Enough to let him go, even though it was difficult."

She flinched. "Loving someone enough to let them go is very

difficult. I know."

He stared at her. "Are you talking about me?"

She didn't answer, but kept staring at Kenley. He was asleep now, his little fist opening and closing as he dreamed.

"I know I violated what you wished from me by coming here tonight," he said.

She glanced at him. "I might have asked you to stay away, but I was so relieved when you came into the room. All I wanted was you, to see you. Just in case."

He swallowed hard. "In case she harmed you in order to take him, you mean."

She nodded.

He pursed his lips at the thought. "Come with me. Let's let him sleep."

"Oh, but—"

He caught her hands and squeezed. "He is sleeping now. Us standing over him having what is surely to be a very important and drawn-out conversation is not best for him. We'll have Nan come in with him, yes?"

She hesitated, because it was clear she feared leaving the boy's side. But he thought there was more to it, as well. But finally she nodded and let him guide her from the room.

Outside Mrs. Barton was coming up the hall, and she smiled. "You found her then, my lord?" she asked.

He stepped forward and quietly told Mrs. Barton a truncated version of what had happened in the nursery. The housekeeper's cheeks paled and she reached over to steady herself on the wall.

"My goodness," she gasped. "How terrifying. What can we do, my lord?"

"Fetch Nan and have her sleep in the room with Kenley tonight rather than her adjoining chamber. And have Mr. Barton step out and raise a hand from the top of the landing. Hopefully that will signal to the guard who has been watching the house this last week and he'll come."

"A guard!" Mrs. Barton gasped, and looked at Phillipa.

"Not a very good one considering what nearly happened here tonight," Rhys muttered.

Phillipa shook her head. "Who would have guessed Rosie would climb up the trellis on the back of the house and climb in through the window? I wouldn't blame him for a lack of that forethought. Obviously I shared in it or I would have been more vigilant about everyone double-checking the sashes."

Rhys glanced at her. Of course she would defend the man. And she wasn't wrong. Her perspective helped to rein in his own, and he so desperately wanted to kiss her in that moment that he had to clench his fists at his sides to control himself.

"When the gentleman comes in, explain what happened and have him begin a perimeter search of the area just to ensure there are no other easy means of access that could be exploited. I do not think that Miss Stanton will return—in fact, I'm almost certain of it. But it will make us all feel better to have something to do."

"Yes, my lord," Mrs. Barton said before she hurried off to do what had been asked of her.

When she was gone, Rhys took Phillipa's hand and led her down the stairs and into the front parlor. He hadn't been here since before moving day, when he'd come alone and stood in the empty place, hoping it would be good for this woman he loved and the child who connected them.

Now he smiled, for in the short time she had lived there, Phillipa had begun to take over. The rooms looked of her, with their bright furniture and piles of books stacked here and there. If he were so lucky as to win her heart tonight, she would take over his home in London too. She would manage his life here and everywhere else they went. She would challenge him and bend him and shape him into a better man just by being...her.

"You are staring at me," she said as she crossed the room away from him to the fire. "I'm sure you have a great deal to say."

He almost laughed as he shut the door behind himself and closed them in together. "I can hardly sort it all out in my head."

She pivoted slowly, and her gaze slid over him from head to toe and then back to his face. She clenched her hands before her and said, "Then allow me to help. Up in the nursery you said something about how you had violated my wishes to come here."

"Yes, you made it very clear that you didn't want me to intrude, to make things harder for you with my presence," he said. "And I know I've broken my promise not to do so."

Her expression softened. "Then why did you do so? You couldn't have known that Rosie would be here, so you didn't come to ride to my rescue. You and I have not spoken for a week...since that last..." Her voice trembled. "...night together before our household moved here. So why did you come, Rhys, unannounced and uninvited, when we have fought so hard not to hurt each other?"

Rhys could hardly breathe as he moved toward her a step. He watched her pupils dilate, desire sparking there alongside the deeper emotions that lined her face. But he also saw her stiffen, steel herself to reject him again because she thought she had to. Because she believed it would protect them both against a storm when they were already in the heart of it.

"Phillipa," he began. "I came here tonight because I've been fighting something for so long. Almost since the first moment I met you, when you looked up at me and my breath just left my lungs."

She squeezed her eyes shut. "Oh, Rhys, please..."

"I can't hold it back anymore. I don't want to." He stepped closer again and she let out the tiniest whimper, like his nearness pained her. But he had to do it. Had to cut in order to heal. "I came here to tell you something that you already know. The same way I know you feel the same. I love you."

She sucked in a harsh breath and he saw her struggling to find words. He found himself glad she couldn't find them yet, because he knew they would be denials. She couldn't accept this, not until he showed her that there was a way.

"God, I love you to my bones, through my blood." He almost

laughed with how true it was. How powerful. "I love all the curves and angles of you, all the courage and weaknesses. Now and forever, today and tomorrow, and there is nothing that will ever change that. Trust me, I have been trying to find a way." He reached for her, but didn't grab her. He just let his fingers trace hers gently. "I *love* you, Phillipa."

P hillipa's mouth dropped open and she heard the little sob that escaped her lips. She felt frozen as she stood there, held steady in his regard, in the absolute certainty of his expression.

She wanted to leap into the arms she knew would be waiting for her. She wanted to throw caution to the wind and accept this beautiful thing she wanted so desperately. But nothing had changed since the last time they made love. Nothing had become better or easier. The barriers still existed and if he could not be strong enough to see them, she had to be.

"You are overwrought thanks to the events of tonight," she said, her tone dull because she couldn't make it anything but when she was denying what her heart desired most. "It has made you forget yourself and all you would lose by loving me."

He arched a brow. "You think you know me so well."

"You know I do."

He smiled, and it seemed so certain that she felt the painful pang of hope. "Well, that part is true even if nothing else you've said is."

"Everything I've said is true," she whispered. "And we've discussed this—"

"Yes. Over and over. Very rationally. But love is not rational. I am mad with it. I cannot leave here without having you know it."

"Lovers," she gasped. "We'll be lovers."

"No." He shook his head firmly. "I want to be your husband. I want to make my life with you, publicly and freely. I want us to raise Kenley as a family, I want our own children to fill our house. I want to love them all equally, as my brother and I weren't. I want you in my arms each night and in my heart every day."

She was wavering. Breaking. He must have known it because he was relentless as he continued, "And I didn't tell you that I loved you because of the threat we faced tonight. Far from it. I rode over here tonight, not having any idea that Rosie would be here."

She shifted. There was no denying that. She had said as much herself a moment before. "And what caused this great change then, if not the fright we both had?"

"It isn't a change," he said. "It isn't new or different. I've loved you for weeks. I've never said it because I've been a coward, stuck thinking I had to row my way out of this storm in only one direction." He smiled. "But tonight I realized, quite suddenly thanks to an intruding and brilliant friend, that there was another way."

She blinked. He sounded so certain, and in that moment she wanted to believe him, even though she knew it wasn't true.

"What other way?" she whispered. "What can erase all the problems being together would solve? What can make it a life free of judgment and pain?"

He drew back a fraction. "Nothing. Even if there were no impediments to our life together, it wouldn't guarantee a life free of pain. Pain is part of the experience. I carry yours, you carry mine, it makes it better, it makes it bearable."

"It will make it worse," she said, "Especially for you. And perhaps you won't grow to hate me for that, but what if I hate myself?"

"In Bath, we had challenges to face," he said. "I locked you out of the work I did, trying to uncover all of Erasmus's bad deeds and I suffered for it. I made myself alone and it was lonely. The moments when I turned to you, when I accepted your pain and shared mine, that was when I was free. Not from the pain, Phillipa, but from the *burden* of it. That is what loving each other does. We don't end the pain, but we make the pain worthwhile. All of it would be worthwhile if I could start my day with you at my side. If I could end my night with you there. If I could cry with you and laugh with you and even argue with you. *That* is living. Without you it would just be...existing."

She stared at him. He was right, of course. These past few days, since the last time they'd been together, she had only been existing. Going through the motions while she longed for him. There hadn't been less pain or suffering or judgment when she left the house. Just less joy and happiness and love because he wasn't there with her.

"Rhys," she whispered, terrified because the door he had just opened was hope. The most dangerous and beautiful creature that had ever existed in this world or any other.

He took the hand he had been stroking and drew her closer, close enough that her body brushed his, and it was like coming home. He was home and he was offering her that forever. "I can't predict the future," he said. "So I can't make promises that our marriage might not make us further pariahs. Or that we might not lose something we can't predict. But we won't lose each other. We won't lose the family we've created, you and me and Kenley."

"And I suppose it follows that losing that family is guaranteed if we walk away," she said.

He nodded slowly. "Take my heart, Phillipa. And my name. And my problems. Give me all of yours. We might not solve them together, but we're going to laugh more and love more and survive better if we are united than if we are separated."

She caught her breath. "How can I deny you? You make it all sound...perfectly imperfect. The fact is that I love you. So deeply and profoundly. When I accepted that you were lost to me, it was as if someone cut off a part of me, something I needed to function. And the moment you walked into the nursery, I was whole again."

She cupped his cheeks and smoothed her thumbs across them. He was warm and whole and hers. He was hers. He smiled because they both knew it. She beamed because the fight was over.

"I love you."

He bent his head and brushed his lips to hers. "Then we cannot do anything but live happily ever after."

EPILOGUE

One Month Later

Autumn leaves swirled on the grassy lawn of Rhys's London garden, and he smiled down from the terrace as he watched Kenley stagger rather drunkenly from Phillipa to Celeste and then to Abigail. He was giggling uproariously as the ladies behaved as though he were the first child to do such a thing.

"They call that walking?" Gilmore said as he and Owen approached, and the duke handed Rhys a drink.

"It *is* walking," Rhys said with a playful glare. "Do not disparage the fact that my son is the most intelligent and amazing child ever to grace this world or I shall meet you at dawn."

Gilmore snorted. "We wouldn't want that." He raised a glass. "To the bride and groom."

"To Pippa and Rhys," Owen said. They clinked glasses and Rhys sipped the amber whisky.

Gilmore asked, "I realize she's been gone a while, but I'm of an untrusting nature, so I will ask again. Do you think you'll have any more trouble with Rosie Stanton?"

"No," Rhys said. "Owen escorted her to the ship himself two days after the unpleasantness at Pippa's old home. She will likely arrive in Lower Canada soon, weather permitting. She has with her an excellent reference from the Earl of Leighton, which will probably carry more weight there than it does here anymore. She promises to send her address once she is settled."

"Lady Leighton intends to keep up her end of the bargain and share information about the child, then?" Gilmore asked, his brows lifting.

"Yes. She would not break such a vow. Nor should she," Rhys said.

Gilmore, pragmatic as he was, didn't look as convinced of that fact as Owen did, or as Rhys felt, but he said nothing and the men went back to watching the ladies.

"From a distance, you know, she is almost bearable," Gilmore said.

Rhys glanced at him from the corner of his eye. "Who?"

"Abigail," Gilmore grunted. "Though now that all is resolved with the situation with Montgomery, I suppose I shall rarely see her anymore."

Owen exchanged a brief glance with Rhys. "That ought to make you very happy."

Gilmore kept his gaze on Abigail for a moment. "Yes. It ought to." He cleared his throat. "I think I shall step inside. Bit of a chill in that wind. I assume the party will join soon."

"I'll join you now," Owen said. "And it looks like the ladies are packing up to come inside, as well."

"I'll wait for Phillipa," Rhys said. "It looks like she's coming up to the terrace while Abigail and Celeste take Kenley in through the lower door."

The others stepped away and that left Rhys, watching as his wife...his *wife*...came up the stairs to the terrace. She was smiling at him. It felt like neither of them had stopped smiling in the fortnight since they wed by special license in his parlor before their friends, one very well-paid and highly judgmental clergyman, and their son.

In the time since, there had been blind pieces in the gossip rags, hisses in the street and one very public speech made about them. And yet, as she glided across the terrace to him, none of that mattered. He had never been happier than he was as she reached him, lifting up on her tiptoes to kiss him deeply.

When they parted, she tilted her head. "Is everything well? You have the strangest expression."

"I was just thinking," he said as he took her arm, "that I am the luckiest man in the whole of England. And that I can't wait until all this riffraff go home so I can show you why."

She giggled as they entered the house, filled with friends and hope and love warm enough to keep out the chill in the wind and in Society.

And all was right with his world.

ENJOY AN EXCERPT OF THE DUKE'S WIFE

THE THREE MRS BOOK 3

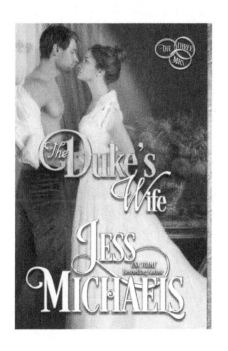

"We should have had three matching red dresses made after what we've all been through this last year. That would be one way to thumb our noses at Society." Abigail Montgomery said with a sigh.

She caught the quick glance her two best friends exchanged behind her and she wished she had not said something so jaded. After all, Celeste and Pippa may have endured much similar humiliations over the last year, they were both happily married now and likely not looking to make the spectacle of themselves that Abigail suddenly wished she could do.

"I think red would be beautiful with your dark hair," Pippa said carefully. "But perhaps a bit much for the first event of the Season after the end of your mourning period."

Abigail rolled her eyes. "Yes, my mourning period."

The year she had been forced to perform the public act of mourning for her husband had been...*interesting* to say the least. Filled with danger and intrigue at the beginning, what with Erasmus's secret marriages to two very women sharing the chamber with her. There had been all kinds of danger that followed. But the year had also contained joy, for she had forged strong bonds with Celeste and Pippa. She'd watched them both find the greatest happiness in new marriages with men who adored them.

The last year of her life had been filled with loneliness, too, because she knew that a happy, romantic ending was not in the cards for her. She had loved Erasmus once...or thought she had. She'd never pictured anything but a long and successful marriage to him. Until he'd destroyed all of it, piece by tiny piece, chipping away until nothing was left. Long before she knew he was a bigamist she had stopped feeling anything for the man but disdain. Knowing he felt the same.

"Are you well, dearest?" Celeste Gregory asked.

That drew Abigail from her maudlin thoughts, and she forced herself to attend. "Of course I'm well. I'm always well. So, the first event of a new Season. What a thrill. And I'm so glad you invited us to see your new gowns, Pippa. They are beautiful."

She forced a tight smile on her face for her friend. Pippa was the new Countess of Leighton and was nervous about the upcoming events of the Spring. With good reason, for her marriage came with a great deal of scandal. She was beautiful. With her mop of unruly blond curls and her bright green eyes, she always looked like a slightly wicked angel. Probably why the Earl of Leighton, Rhys, adored her so much. The exterior matched the interior.

"You are certainly going to impress," Abigail mused.

Pippa had been holding up a gown with an elaborately stitched bodice that would clung to her curves just so and a fall of a slighter paler silk that made up the skirt. "I hope so," she sighed. "Appearances mean so much to the ton."

"That green matches your eyes perfectly!" Celeste cooed.

"Rhys picked the fabric," Pippa said with a blush and a happy smile. She had been married to the man just over six months and it seemed there was no dimming of the spark between them. And for Pippa, Abigail was very happy. There were no other, less pleasant emotions that tightened her chest. Not even a one.

"Well, it's as pretty as all the rest," Celeste said, clasping her hands before her. "You will be the belle of any ball."

Pippa's smile faded slightly. "I don't know about that," she said. "I look forward to the first event of the Season. Well, the first event for Rhys and I...but I think it doesn't bode well that we haven't been invited to any others. That we must host our own fete in order to make ourselves known."

Abigail caught Pippa's hands and squeezed gently, her own troubles pushed to the background for a moment. "The way Society views your relationship to Rhys is...complicated."

"I know. Had I been legally married to Erasmus, I never even would have been allowed for me to marry Rhys."

"Yes," Abigail mused. "Ecclesiastic law does frown upon a woman marrying her dead husband's brother. But you were *not* legally married, so that eliminates that problem."

Pippa shrugged. "Somewhat. But the scandal of Erasmus's bigamy and the fact that I *did* marry his brother and become countess has not lessened all the burden Rhys must bear."

"You relieve his burdens, not add to them," Celeste insisted. "He's said as much to Owen many times. He has never regretted marrying you."

"Nor I him," Pippa said, tears leaping to her eyes. "But I do fear that we will not find acceptance. I am not from his world, not truly, but I can see that it matters to him. It matters how the world sees us, for our sake and for the sake of Kenley and any children we might be happy enough to have together in the future."

Abigail stiffened at the mention of Kenley Montgomery. He was the child Erasmus had sired with yet another woman in his life. The one who had ultimately murdered him. Pippa and Rhys had taken the little boy in and were raising him as if he were their own. He was a happy, bright child and Abigail enjoyed seeing him a great deal. Even if he did create yet another reminder of how little her late husband had given a damn about anyone but himself.

"It is very complicated," Abigail said. "And scandalous. But time will soften it. Rhys is well liked and respected by many important people. This Season and even the next may be difficult, but eventually another scandal, perhaps even a more shocking one will happen and *they* will all shift their ire. Be strong for Rhys and for yourself and know that you are not alone. You have an army of friends and allies behind you."

"That is true." Pippa's face lit up slightly. "Of course you and Owen and Celeste will be there tomorrow, Harriet has agreed to come with Lena, and that will make an enormous splash since anyone who is anyone wants to be a member of their salon."

Abigail shifted. "Have you considered that you might wish to rescind the kind invitation to me?"

Pippa's eyes went wide. "Why would I ever do that?"

"I am the legal wife," she said softly. "If you wish to disconnect your own reputation from Erasmus's, having me there will do nothing to make that happen."

Pippa and Celeste exchanged a glance filled with meaning, and then they both stepped up to her. She was wrapped in their mutual embrace, and for a moment she felt the urge to sag into it. Collapse against them and let them be her strength. Her own, after all, had felt like it was waning for some time.

But she didn't. She had never been the kind to collapse or ask for help. So she straightened her shoulders instead and shook her head. "Gracious, I don't know what I've done to deserve such affection."

"Just being you," Pippa said as they both stepped away. "And you are ridiculous if you think I don't want and need you at our party. When we rise, we will rise together. I'll hear nothing more on the subject."

"As you say," Abigail said, and was pleased her voice didn't tremble with the emotions that this unwavering support created in her.

She did adore these two women. If Erasmus had to betray her as he had, at least she was unwaveringly happy in his choices.

"Anyway, those Rhys has invited will create a lot of acceptance," Pippa continued. "I know he's mentioned Lord and Lady Goffard, the Earl of Yarrowood, the Duke of Gilmore, Sir William Livingston—"

Abigail pursed her lips and pivoted to pace to the fireplace. "You tried to gloss over Gilmore, you wicked thing. But of course Rhys is inviting him." She rolled her eyes. "Why in the world would such a good and decent man associate himself with such a…such a…cretin?"

She glanced over her shoulder to see Celeste and Pippa exchanging yet another of those loaded looks. A world of communication flowed between them, and all of it was about Abigail. Her cheeks heated and she hated herself for creating this situation. Hated the Duke of Gilmore even more for it.

Horrible man.

"Gilmore is my husband's best friend—he has been for decades," Pippa said, Abigail thought a little gently.

"He has become one of Owen's, as well," Celeste said softly. "I still don't understand why you hate him so."

Abigail let out a gasp of annoyance. "You don't? I don't understand why all of you don't despise him. He inserted himself into the situation with Erasmus—"

"*You* inserted him into the situation when you wrote him that anonymous letter telling him that our horrible shared husband was trying to make Gilmore's sister into wife number four," Pippa interrupted.

Abigail folded her arms. That was true. She had done that, there was no pretending otherwise.

"He...he deserved to know the truth," she said, softer this time. "He deserved a chance to save his sister if he could, and he did. I am happy that he did." She cleared her throat past the sudden lump that had formed there. "However, he doesn't know the letter writer was me and I never want him to know. The fact remains that instead of just protecting his sister and then staying out of it, he made everything worse. He hired the investigator, he starting stirring the pot, and everything came out because of it."

"Everything was going to come out regardless," Celeste said. "And I'm rather happy Gilmore hired *the investigator*, considering I married him."

Abigail bent her head. "I'm making a muck of this. Of course I'm happy Owen came and helped us all and that you two fell in love. I just...Gilmore is an arrogant, frustrating...and he's competitive..."

"You're competitive!" both of her friends said at once, and then laughed.

"I'm competitive in a *good* way," Abigail insisted.

Celeste and Pippa were smothering smiles, and that only made all this worse. Any time she talked about Gilmore, it was worse. After all, when she listed his negative qualities, whether out loud or to herself, she also couldn't help but add that he was handsome. Very handsome. Too handsome. With those broad shoulders and that defined jaw and those dark brown eyes that seemed to pierce a person to their very soul.

Why couldn't he have been less appealing? Then hating him somehow would have been easier.

Pippa shook her head. "I am sorry you feel this way, Abigail. I can only imagine how difficult it is to constantly have to cross paths with someone you dislike so strongly."

Abigail nodded. Though she and Gilmore hadn't crossed paths all that often recently. Not since the intimate gathering to celebrate Pippa and Rhys's wedding months ago. Abigail had been sequestered in her "mourning" and Gilmore had been...

Well, she knew he'd been at his estate in Cornwall over the winter. Far, far away from her.

"Perhaps the best thing you can do is to avoid him," Celeste suggested.

Abigail swallowed. "Yes. I think that will be the best. Certainly he dislikes me as much as I dislike him, so it will be easy enough to do so."

With that subject resolved, at least in their estimation, Pippa and Celeste went back to examining the rest of Pippa's new gowns. But though Abigail still nodded and interjected, her mind now took her to the very unpleasant Duke of Gilmore.

Avoiding him was never easy. For some reason they always stumbled into each other's paths. But it truly was for the best. After all, returning to Society was going to be hard enough. She didn't need Gilmore's interference. She didn't need him besting her in the game they had been playing since the first moment she laid eyes on him.

ALSO BY JESS MICHAELS

The Three Mrs

The Unexpected Wife

The Defiant Wife

The Duke's Wife

The Duke's By-Blows

The Love of a Libertine

The Heart of a Hellion

The Matter of a Marquess

The Redemption of a Rogue

The 1797 Club

The Daring Duke

Her Favorite Duke

The Broken Duke

The Silent Duke

The Duke of Nothing

The Undercover Duke

The Duke of Hearts

The Duke Who Lied

The Duke of Desire

The Last Duke

The Scandal Sheet

The Return of Lady Jane

Stealing the Duke

Lady No Says Yes

My Fair Viscount

Guarding the Countess

The House of Pleasure

Seasons

An Affair in Winter

A Spring Deception

One Summer of Surrender

Adored in Autumn

The Wicked Woodleys

Forbidden

Deceived

Tempted

Ruined

Seduced

Fascinated

The Notorious Flynns

The Other Duke

The Scoundrel's Lover

The Widow Wager

No Gentleman for Georgina

A Marquis for Mary

To see a complete listing of Jess Michaels' titles, please visit:

http://www.authorjessmichaels.com/books

ABOUT THE AUTHOR

USA Today Bestselling author Jess Michaels likes geeky stuff, Vanilla Coke Zero, anything coconut, cheese, fluffy cats, smooth cats, any cats, many dogs and people who care about the welfare of their fellow humans. She is lucky enough to be married to her favorite person in the world and lives in the heart of Dallas, TX where she's trying to eat all the amazing food in the city.

When she's not obsessively checking her steps on Fitbit or trying out new flavors of Greek yogurt, she writes historical romances with smoking hot alpha males and sassy ladies who do anything but wait to get what they want. She has written for numerous publishers and is now fully indie and loving every moment of it (well, almost every moment).

Jess loves to hear from fans! So please feel free to contact her at Jess@AuthorJessMichaels.com.

Jess Michaels raffles a gift certificate EVERY month to members of her newsletter, so sign up on her website:
http://www.AuthorJessMichaels.com/

facebook.com/JessMichaelsBks
twitter.com/JessMichaelsBks
instagram.com/JessMichaelsBks
bookbub.com/authors/jess-michaels